The Strong Tower

By

Ronna M. Bacon

Verses
Psalm 61:3
For You have been a shelter for me, A strong tower from the enemy.

Proverbs 18:10. The name of the Lord is a strong tower; The righteous run to it and are safe.
New King James Version

For my mom, who believed in my dream to write a novel enough to say, "Why don't you?" and shared a love of reading with me. Luv you. Miss you.

Table of Contents

Angry words filled the air of the house as the two men faced off against each other, both determined the other would back down. Neither budged from their position.

Eyes glaring, the younger man pushed at the man standing in front of him, accusing him of theft. He was out money and he wanted what he felt he was owed.

The older man shook his head. He didn't have the money that was demanded. He had hidden it well and it wouldn't be found unless he wanted it to. He was regretting getting involved with this man. He knew better but the chance to make a lot of money had won.

He turned his back as the younger man continued his rant. He reached for his hat, intending on walking away and not looking back. He would go somewhere no one knew him. Out west would work. He'd change his name and his occupation.

He didn't see the young man pick up the knife and rush towards him, anger streaming from his face. A sudden thrust with the knife and the man lay still, his life blood seeping from him. The younger man stood over him, his fist clenched around the knife before he stared down at the knife and then the body laying in front of him. He turned to the man laying there and looked around. He needed to get rid of the body.

He turned searching and then studied the wall behind him. It had been framed and was ready for the drywall. These friends of the older man were renovating. He had offered to help, not expecting HIM to show up. He ran for the garage, finding the tools he wanted and the drywall sitting there. Dragging sheets of drywall into the house, he looked down at the man on the floor. He dragged the man over and lifting him, stuffed him inside, searching him first for anything in his pockets. He quickly boarded up the wall, and then stared at the rug. A few quick movements and the rug was gone. He swept the room for anything that would identify either one of them and then ran for his car, speeding away, leaving nothing behind he hoped would incriminate him. If anyone asked, he was at home all evening, all by himself, with the television on. Tomorrow, he'd visit the local landfill site and get rid of both the knife and the carpet, as well as the

clothes he was wearing. The only thing was,
he didn't know where the money was hidden
and now he'd never know.

Chapter 1

$\mathscr{B}$lowing out a breath, MaKenna Dunne stared around her backyard. The windstorm that had swept through in the night had been violent and damaging. She stared at the branches strewn around her yard and sighed. She couldn't clean this up on her own, she was sure. And she certainly was not going to call in her brother, Riordan. He had been against her buying this small house with all the trees, warning her of just such an event. Besides, he lived two hours away from her. She turned and trudged back to her home, a small bungalow, just big enough for her and her Shetland Sheepdog, Emma. Emma trotted around her, her sable coat shining in the bright early morning light.

She dreaded having to call anyone. The man that had appeared at her door last night had gotten rather loud and violent. She shuddered, her hand going to her wrist as she rubbed at the bruises. He won't take no for an answer, that she wasn't letting him into her house. She had had to repair the damage to her railing where he had shoved at it, knocking it off the base. She had swept up the broken pottery too, where he had thrown her pots from the front porch. She hadn't called in the police. That was a last resort only. The fear still coursed through her. She touched her face where his hand had landed, slapping her hard enough that she had fallen in the front door. But that was yesterday, wasn't it? He wouldn't be back.

Thinking it was good that it was Saturday and she didn't have to be at work, she slipped off her shoes before heading into her kitchen, her eyes searching for her phone. Now, where had she put it? She didn't have a habit of keeping it in a pocket or even nearby. She finally found it on the table in the living room and scrolled through her contacts, finding the one she wanted. Hearing a noise outside, she dialed even as she walked to the front door, fear coursing through her, frowning as she saw the truck sitting in her driveway. The driver, a man around her own age, she decided, was heading for her door.

She stepped back from the window as her friend, Beth, answered.

"MaKenna, I was just about to call you. Did you have a lot of damage?" Beth always spoke in a rush, as if there was only so much time to do what she needed to do.

"There is, Beth. I called to see if you knew if your brother would be in town today and had time to come out and look at the limbs in my backyard." The ringing doorbell distracted her for a moment. "I'm sorry, what do you say?"

"I talked to him about twenty minutes ago. He asked about you. I told him you wouldn't call Riordan. He's on his way over."

"I guess, then, that's who rang my doorbell. Call you later. We need to do coffee soon."

"We do. Get through today and we'll talk tomorrow. How about lunch after church?"

Agreeing to that, MaKenna pocketed her phone, drew a deep breath, and opened the door. The man standing there turned, watching her carefully before he spoke.

"You're MaKenna? I'm Beth's brother, Ciaran Quinn." He studied her reaction for a moment, a puzzled frown on his face, seeing the fear lurking just below the surface. "Beth said you wouldn't call your brother, but that you likely had limbs down in your yard."

"Thank you. I am MaKenna, and it's nice to meet you. Beth has spoken of you often. Come on through. Emma, stay."

His eyes shot to her face before he realized she was talking to an animal. His eyes dropped to the dog standing between the two of them, eyes watchful.

He followed her, keeping his eyes on the dog. Dogs did not get along with him, or he didn't get along with dogs. It had been like that all his life. Emma seemed to be assessing him, her brown eyes seeing far more than he ever thought a dog would see.

He stared around the yard behind the house, taking in the number of limbs that had fallen.

"You've had a lot come down. Not a lot of large ones, thankfully. I can clear this up in no time for you, if you wish."

MaKenna turned to study the man standing beside her. Tall, well over six foot, she thought, red gold curls and deep blue eyes, crinkles at the corner as if he laughed or smiled a lot. The deep tan showed a liking for the outdoors. She nodded, even as she had to will the fear rising within her back down.

"I can help. There's a fire lane running behind the house and a gate in the back fence if you want to move your truck back there."

Riordan turned, taking in the golden hair and amber eyes of the woman, no, lady, he thought, standing beside him. Beth had been trying for months to introduce them, but he had resisted and right now he couldn't think of why. He knew from Beth that MaKenna had had difficulty a while ago with an old boyfriend but she hadn't said anything about that lately.

By noon, the yard had been cleared. Riordan searched for any missing branches, then paused, his hand reaching for a small metal box. It was rusty as if it had been out in the elements for years, battered, but still intact. He turned it over in his hands before heading towards MaKenna.

"MaKenna, I found this in your backyard. Is it yours?"

MaKenna turned, frowning as she took the box. "No, it's not. I've never seen it before."

Ciaran watched as she turned the box over and tried to open it. "Here. I have something in the truck that might be able to open. It's not that big, is it?"

She shrugged as she followed him, still trying to puzzle it out. "It's strange, you know. Do you think it was stuck in one of the branches?"

He shrugged himself as he pulled a tool box to him and then reached for a flat head screw driver.

"It could have been, especially if you've never seen it before." He carefully worked to open it, surprised at the key that fell out.

"This is really strange, isn't it?" She reached for the key as a shadow fell over them. She spun staring at the man standing there behind them.

Ciaran moved so he was standing between them, his stance protective. "Can we help you?"

The man nodded. "I think I'll take that box, young man. It doesn't belong to you."

Ciaran fisted his hand around the box. "I don't think so. It doesn't belong to you either." He heard quiet movement from MaKenna and hoped she was putting the key in her pocket.

Sudden movement from the man, and Ciaran was flat on his back, his eyes closed, the box in the man's hand. MaKenna jumped and screamed, her eyes darting between the two men.

"You've been warned. We'll be back for what we want from you." The harsh angry words spit at her and she drew back, but not before a shove sent her into the tailgate of Ciaran's truck, leaving her crumpled on the ground, her hand gripping her side.

Fear in her eyes, she watched the man run from them. Lord, what did I just get mixed up in, she wondered. I've never had this before and I don't like it.

Hearing a groan, she dropped to her knees beside Ciaran, her hand touching his face.

"Ciaran? Can you hear me?"

Ciaran's eyes fluttered open, and he squinted as if the light hurt.

"What happened?" He sat up with her help, his hand to his jaw, face tight with pain.

"Whoever that was, he took the box. And he threatened to come back." She stared at the path the assailant had taken. "I have no idea what they want."

Ciaran stood, his eyes on her, then following her line of sight. "I'm sure they'll be back. How did he know about the box, anyway? And you did say they?"

MaKenna shivered, her hands running up and down her arms. "I have no idea. It was pretty old, wasn't it? But, that could explain it. And yes I did. There was another man waiting at the end of the laneway. I think he's the same one who was here last night." Fear shaded her voice, causing Ciaran to look at her.

"Explain what?" Ciaran asked as he closed up the toolbox and shoved it back to its place in the truck bed and slammed the tailgate shut.

"I've felt like I've been watched and Emma has sensed someone in the yard. When I've been out with her, she'll go through the house as if someone has been in there, but nothing is disturbed."

Ciaran spun to stare down at her, his thoughts racing as to the danger she was in. He could see the fear in her eyes and in her stance.

"Come on, MaKenna. I know I'm still a relative stranger to you, but show me what you mean."

MaKenna shook her head, even as she stared at her home. "There's nothing to show, that's the thing. Just Emma being Emma, showing me that something was off about the house. She does that, you know? I trust her more than I trust another person. Does that make sense?"

Ciaran stared at her. He had never heard anyone say that before. "I'm really not sure what to say, MaKenna."

She nodded, knowing that she had lost him somewhere along the line. She sighed. As always lately, it was just her and her dog.

Chapter 2

MaKenna stood the following Wednesday in her doorway, her arms cradling Emma. She had gone out for a walk and returned to find her front door wide open, the lock broken. She sighed, walking away from the door, and reaching for her phone. She had to call this in; she had no choice. Fear resonated through her. She couldn't imagine who had done this. She didn't have much of value, just starting out. The one thing she considered the most important to her was right there with her, her dog.

Beth found her seated on her lawn, Emma laying on her crossed legs, as she watched the activity in and around her house.

Dropping down beside her friend, Beth reached to hug her, backing off when Emma growled. "Emma! You know me!" Her startled eyes met MaKenna's.

"She's upset, Beth. She does this when she thinks I need protecting." She rubbed the dog's ears, relishing the softness of the fur.

"What happened?"

"I came home to a broken down door. And now that it's after hours, I can't get it fixed until morning." Tears pooled near the surface of her eyes.

"Wait. I can call Ciaran. I'm sure he'd have a door in his shop."

"No, don't. He's done enough." MaKenna spoke quickly, trying to forestall what she knew her friend was up to.

Beth was already speaking with her brother. As she pocketed her phone, she commented, "He's on his way. He said he had a door he could put in for you as well as new locks. Is that really my brother?"

MaKenna stared at her friend, trying to understand what she really meant. "He doesn't do this?"

Beth shook her head. "Not usually. So, what happened on Saturday?" She stared at her friend as MaKenna shrugged.

"Nothing. He cleaned up my yard and that's it."

"I don't think so. But you can keep your secret."

Beth walked the yard, her eyes on her friend, her thoughts muddled. Something more had happened on Saturday, more than what either of them were saying. She watched as Ciaran walked towards her.

"Beth? What happened?"

She turned to find MaKenna. "I have no idea. She came home to that."

"And Emma?" He searched for the dog, finding her tight to MaKenna's leg where she stood taking to the patrol officer.

"She was out with MaKenna. What happened on Saturday?" Her eyes searched her brother's. "She says nothing did, you won't talk, but you have the faintest bruise on your face. And don't tell it was an accident. You're too careful. And MaKenna is trying to hide the bruises on her wrist."

Ciaran sighed, knowing he couldn't keep it from his younger sister. "We found a metal box with a key in it. MaKenna still has the key, but someone approached us, knocked me down, and took the box." Then he spun. "Bruises? I didn't notice them. That's strange."

"Knocked you down?" Her voice rose, then was silent as she clapped a hand to her mouth. "Ciaran!"

He shrugged as he pointed towards MaKenna. "Don't tell her you know. I need you to do that for me."

She nodded even as Ciaran moved towards MaKenna.

MaKenna turned slightly as she heard footsteps approaching, her heart racing. She finished her conversation with the patrol officer and waited.

"MaKenna?" Ciaran's quiet question reached her.

"Ciaran. Beth shouldn't have called you." She refused to look at him, hoping he would just go away.

"Yes, she should have. I can repair your door and put on new locks. You know I'm a renovator, that's what I do for a living." He stood waiting for her to speak.

She stood, arms crossed over her abdomen, a blank look on her face. She stared at the onlookers, a frown replacing the look.

"Ciaran, he's here again."

"Who?"

"That man from Saturday. He's standing behind your truck. What do they think I have?"

Ciaran turned to face his truck. The man standing there tipped an imaginary hat before turning and walking away, smirking at them as he did so.

"I have no idea. Are the police done yet?"

She nodded. "They couldn't find any evidence of anyone in the house, but they said there was some stuff tossed as they called it. Now, I have to go in and go through my place."

"I'll walk through with you. Leave Emma with Beth." He peeked around her at his sister, who nodded and reached for the leash.

MaKenna walked slowly up to the door, took a deep breath and stepped inside, her hands going to her mouth.

"What on?"

She heard Ciaran behind her. "Some stuff tossed?"

She stood for a moment, then walked through. "Why? What do they think I have?" She spun as she neared the kitchen, staring back at her living room.

Books were tossed from the built-in book shelves and the shelves themselves were broken from the wall. She looked towards the bedroom, then hesitantly walked that way. The three bedrooms had been tossed as well. The one she used for an office was the worst. Papers had been thrown all over. Her computer was still there, turned off as it usually was.

Ciaran spoke from behind her. "Let's put Emma in the back yard, and then Beth can come help you. I'll work on replacing your door."

She nodded, tears near the surface, trying to calm herself before she spoke.

"Why, Ciaran? Is it something to do with that key? I don't know of any hidden places here."

He shrugged. "It might be, but let's take one step at a time." He watched as she physically calmed herself and then turned to her office, shutting off her emotions. Lord, I have no idea what's going on here but You do. Use my hands to help her today. Calm her.

Beth stood watching her friend, then turned to stare at her brother. Was what had happened on Saturday really at the root of this?

"Beth, can you come here for a moment?" MaKenna's voice called from her bedroom.

"What is it?" Beth stopped as MaKenna held up some photos. "What did they do?"

"These aren't mine. They were on the closet floor. I have no idea who these people are. But I need to get up to the ceiling there. There seems to be a crack of some kind."

Beth stepped back to the hall and spoke with Ciaran, who spun, staring at her, then headed out for a ladder.

"Where's the crack, MaKenna?"

She pointed, and positioning the ladder, he climbed up to look. "Do you have a flashlight?"

She handed him one and waited as he pried at the ceiling, ducking as layers of disturbed dust fell. Beth started to giggle at the sight her brother made and he glared at her before his hands were reaching into the cavity, handing down photos and letters to MaKenna.

"I'll take these to the kitchen." MaKenna shot a look at the clock. "You two had your Bible study tonight and it's already started. I shouldn't have called you." Panic traced through her words as she began to pace.

Beth shook her head and spoke, but Makenna ignored her. She stared at her brother, who stood, a puzzled look on his face. He pointed towards the living room and Beth nodded.

Ciaran approached her, finally stopping her frantic pacing with hands on her upper arms. He could see her drawing deep breaths to calm herself even though she wouldn't look up at him.

"MaKenna, it's okay. We didn't need to be there tonight. God understands. He knew you needed us instead." He finally got through the fog filtering through her brain.

She stood for a moment, her eyes searching his. "I'm sorry, Ciaran. It's just been so overwhelming. I thought…". Whatever she thought went unspoken as the doorbell rang. Ciaran stopped her before she could head that way.

"Let me. You're in no shape right now to speak with anyone. How be you make us some coffee or something?"

She snorted. "Or something? And just what would that be?"

He grinned as he turned and walked towards the front of the house, opening the door to find an older gentleman standing there, a frown on his face.

"What's the meaning of making me wait?" He tried to shove his way inside, but Ciaran blocked him.

"And you might be?"

"I could ask you the same thing. Just who are you?"

"A friend of the homeowner's. So, who are you?"

The man stopped, staring at Ciaran, then past him at MaKenna as she stood in the hallway watching.

"I'm sorry. I have no idea who you are. So I suggest you leave, or I will call the police." MaKenna's voice was calm but there was an undertone in it that caused the man to step away from the door, muttering.

"What did you say?" Ciaran stepped towards him, fists forming, a protective instinct rising within him.

"None of your business." The man shot one more glare at MaKenna and then turned and walked away.

Ciaran followed, not seeing a vehicle. He motioned for Beth to lock the door and made his way to the sidewalk, watching as the man stormed down the street and then around the corner. Puzzled, Ciaran debating about following him but decided the two women needed his protection more.

"What was that about, Ciaran?" MaKenna stood on the steps, waiting for him.

"MaKenna, what part of staying behind a locked door don't you get?" His words were harsher than she expected.

"Ciaran? Just who was that?"

He shook his head as he grasped her arm, turned her and almost shoved her into the house. "I don't know, MaKenna. That's why I wanted you to stay inside, behind the door, which Beth had locked. For all we knew, he was part of the group who trashed your house"

She paled, her hand going to her mouth. "Do you really think so?"

"I have no idea, and you just put yourself into danger by coming out like that." Frustrated, Ciaran ran his hands through his hair, disturbing the dust and the cobwebs. "Listen, did you get the coffee made?"

"I did, but I don't have anything I can get ready in a hurry for you to eat."

"That's okay. I ordered pizza." Beth waved her phone at them. "Let's work away until it comes, and then I think we'll need to call it a night."

Ciaran nodded, his eyes on MaKenna. "Do you have somewhere you can lock away what we found?"

She nodded, turned to her office. "I do." She reached for a panel, revealing a safe. "I had this put in after I moved in. Here, let's put it all in here."

Ciaran stood, mouth open, as he watched her stick the papers away, before turning back to the living room. What would have caused her to have a safe built and hidden away?

"MaKenna. I'll rebuild your shelves for you, but first, I would like to check out the walls." He stopped as Beth headed for the door and their pizzas. "Let's eat, then plan. I'll have to take some measurements as well to work out what materials are needed."

Chapter 3

MaKenna stared at the paper on the door of her work the next morning. Closed until further notice. Now what, she thought. She hadn't received a phone call from her boss that he wouldn't be in. She heard footsteps beside her and the young receptionist, Anna, stood there.

"What's going on?" She yanked at the door. "It's locked."

"It is very locked and the office is closed. Did you know anything about it?"

Anna shook her head. "No, everything seemed fine when I left yesterday just after you. Did you try your key?"

MaKenna shook her head. "No, I just got here. Let's see if it still works."

She was surprised when she opened the door and stepped inside. The office had been trashed, just like her home. She paused, turning to Anna. "I don't like this, Anna. I'm calling in the police."

                    ☆ ☆ ☆ ☆ ☆

Two hours later, Anna turned to her. "Do you think it will be much longer?"

MaKenna shook her head. "I have no idea. You can leave if you want. Just make sure the patrol officer has your contact information." She debated about leaving as well. "I think I'll head out too."

"Before you leave, Miss Dunne, I would like to speak with you. Miss Evans, leave me your information and I'll be in touch."

MaKenna turned as a burly police detective pointed towards the picnic table under the spreading maple trees, his light brown hair blowing in the soft breeze, his gray eyes studying her.

"Let's sit. It's been a busy day already and it's not even half over." He wiped at the sweat on his forehead with a shirt sleeve.

MaKenna sat facing the detective, giving a quiet thanks as she was handed a bottle of water.

"First, let me clarify. This is just a preliminary interview. I'm Detective Art Bourne. I understand you've been here in town about six months?"

"That's correct. It's a small town, Oakton, and that's what I wanted. I love the lake and when this opportunity to work came up, I couldn't resist moving here to be near Lake Erie."

He nodded, jotting down entries in his note pad.

"Now about today. What time did you arrive?"

"About 8:55, just like always. We open at 9, so I'm always a little early. That's when I found the note on the door. That's unlike Dr. Stirling. He would have called."

Art watched the struggle going on in the woman seated across from him.

"So, then. Where is he?" MaKenna finally looked at the detective.

"We don't know, but we are concerned. We found blood in his office. Enough for us to worry about his safety." His keen eyes studied her, watching for her reaction.

MaKenna paled. "Blood?" She began to shake. "That's not good. Why did I ever move here, take this position of medical office assistant? Riordan was right."

"Excuse me?" The detective was puzzled, his eyes rising to watch over her head.

"My brother told me not to move here. I should have listened." She stood. "Is that all for now?"

"It is. You've left your contact information with the officer? Then you can leave. I'll be in touch for further questions."

"And it's a don't leave town order, is it?"

He grinned for a moment before sobering. "Not at all. We just need to know where you are so we can continue our conversation. There'll be many conversations, Miss Dunne." He watched her, sensing there was more to her fear than just what had happened that day.

"I don't like the sounds of that." She walked away, her strides even and fluid.

Early evening, a knock came to her door, and she hesitated about answering. When she heard her name, she rose from the couch and headed to unlock the door and let Ciaran in, before turning and seating herself again, reaching for the paperwork they had found.

"Are you okay?" Ciaran was concerned.

She shrugged. "How can I be? My boss is missing, there was blood in his office, and my work is shut down."

He studied her for a moment before he sighed and then sat across from her, reaching for the photos, opting not to push her any more than he had.

"What have you found out so far?"

"That I don't know these people at all. Is that good enough?" Her answer was abrupt and almost snappish.

"MaKenna, I didn't do this to you. So hold the curtness, okay?" He waited until she raised her eyes to him. "I know you're hurting, but don't take it out on me. I'm only trying to help." He threw the photos down and stood. "But it seems as if you don't want help."

MaKenna watched as he walked away, her thoughts in a jumble. No, she really didn't need him, now did she? She had been just fine on her own, and she would continue to be that way. Right, Lord, I don't need anyone in my life. It causes too many complications. She shut her heart off from listening and picked up the paperwork again, before throwing it down.

Heading for the backyard, she searched for Emma, picking up her frisbee to throw for her. But she had no interest in that either. What was going through her mind that she couldn't concentrate?

A text message alert startled her enough to almost drop her phone as she pulled it out. She read it and then sighed. Anna and she would have a lot of work to do over the next few days, canceling appointments and tests until such time as a new physician would or could even be found. She wondered if she would be needing to move on to another town, to find another position. The thing of it was, she loved her small town, the people, the proximity to the lake, just the feeling of being free and able to make all her own decisions. It was a feeling hard fought for, and she wouldn't give it up without a fight. She turned to head back to her house, her steps hesitating for a moment. She had heard something, a voice whispering to her. She spun, not seeing anything, but knowing someone had been there. Emma stood, her hackles raised, a low growl emanating from her, her eyes on the back of the yard.

Chapter 4

Ciaran stepped back from the trim he was installing around a doorway to see who was calling for him, then stepped forward again, the nail hammer sending out little puffs of air as he used it. He made sure the safety was on before laying it down and walking towards his sister, a puzzled look on his face. She shouldn't be here at this time of the morning. He glanced as his watch as he stopped in front of her.

"Beth? Are you supposed to be at work?" His sister ran a bookstore and was always at work at this time.

She nodded, her arms wrapped around her abdomen, her eyes darting around, not looking at him until he touched her shoulder. "I should be but I had some errands to run. I needed to talk to you." She paced, wringing her hands as she did so.

Ciaran finally pulled her into a hug, the only way he knew how to stop her when she was like this. "Okay, sis. What's up?"

She sighed. "Have you talked to MaKenna? It's been a week and she won't return my calls or text messages. I'm worried."

"She won't? I talked to her the day she found her workplace broken into, but not since. She didn't seem to want to talk to anyone."

Beth nodded, before walking back outside, Ciaran trailing behind her. "I called her brother. Riordan says this is what she'll do. She'll shut down and push everyone away. He's going to try and get down tomorrow, but he wasn't sure if he even could. The church he pastors has an event that he needs to be at."

Ciaran blew out a breath, already knowing where Beth was going with the conversation. "We can't force her to talk to us, you know. Just keep doing what you're doing. You've stopped by her place? And she wouldn't answer?"

"No. She wouldn't. I was even sure she was home. I could hear Emma barking."

Ciaran sighed. "Okay, I'll stop by after work. I have the materials I need to repair her shelves. That is, if she'll let me."

"What?" Beth stared at him, waiting for him to explain himself.

Ciaran shook his head. "Never mind. Go on back to your store. If that photography book has come in, set it aside for me."

"It already is. You just need to stop by."

Ciaran watched as his sister drove way, then raised his eyes to study the surrounding homes. He felt watched, but he could never see anyone. And feelings weren't enough to go to the police with, even though his best friend from childhood was an officer on the force.

MaKenna stood on her front steps that night, watching as Ciaran walked towards her. She dangled the watering can from her fingers. She wanted to work in her gardens tonight, needing to feel the dirt under her fingers, but it didn't look as if she would be. She wasn't happy and she knew she needed to change her attitude. She had seen a car following her for the last few days and that worried her.

"Ciaran. What are you doing here?" Her voice was less than welcoming and she sighed, knowing it had come out wrong.

Ciaran stopped, his eyes assessing her. "I have the material for your shelves. You know? The ones that were ripped out? The ones I said I would fix for you?"

Her eyes slid shut. "I'm sorry. It's been a bad few days at work. I shouldn't take it out on you. Come in, then."

Ciaran followed her in, his eyes taking in the piles of books on the floor and the papers on the coffee table. "Have you been working with those papers?"

She shook her head. "No, I haven't. I've been so tired after dealing with stuff at work, that I haven't felt like it. We have a new physician coming in to take over for now, a locum you call it, and it's always tough."

"I'm glad you still have your work." He looked around again, a frown on his face. "You got rid of the old shelving?"

"It's in the garage. I couldn't leave it in here with Emma."

He nodded, then walked over to the wall where the book shelves had been, feeling along it.

"This is strange, MaKenna. This wall is thicker than what you would expect. The shelves run the length of it, are not inset, with

gaps at the ends, so it shouldn't be this thick."
He turned as he heard a sound from her.

She stared at the wall, then at him, before spinning and almost running to her office. He waited, then followed, watching as she pulled more papers from the safe.

"That must be what this is then. See?" She thrust the paper at him. "Look. Is that what I think it is? Wasn't there a safe or something there at one time?" She handed him the papers she had selected, pointing to a particular photo.

He studied her for a moment, then grasped the papers, looking at what she had pointed to. He spun, moving to where he could stare at the wall. "I think you're onto something here, MaKenna. Did you ever track down any of the previous owners?"

She shook her head. "This was an estate sale. The owner had no living relatives that I know of. The lawyer I had seemed to think he was the last in his family. Finding a family member would have been helpful, now wouldn't it?"

"It would. I wonder if there are any friends left in town. I remember the male. He taught school for years before he retired." He stared at the wall and then back at the papers. "I think there might be something behind the wall, but it would mean tearing out the complete wall. But…". His voice died away. "You put the old shelving out in the garage?"

She nodded. "Here. Through this door. Go on ahead. I just need to let Emma in and feed her."

Ciaran stared around her garage, noting the tools she had hung up. Not what he would have expected, to see carpentry tools and plumbing tools. Someone was handy, he thought. Then, spying the wood, he walked over, walking around it to study the pile. He didn't see anything overt there, but that didn't mean there wasn't something. He would have to study each piece, he knew.

MaKenna paused beside him, her eyes going from the wood to his face and back again.

"It's not going to move itself, you know." Her eyes sparkled with mirth.

He laughed. "No, it's not. I'm just trying to determine how best to handle this. Do you have a camera? If we take pictures as we go along, then we'll know what we have and haven't done."

She sighed. "I do, but I've already looked over each piece pretty carefully and didn't see anything."

"You did, huh? Find anything odd."

She shook her head. "Nothing. No markings. No writings. Nothing." She returned to the living room, Ciaran trailing after her. "Just this wall."

Ciaran nodded, knowing that sometimes old homes hid things. He walked over to the wall, feeling along it once more, a frown on his face.

"I still think this is thicker than it should be." He turned to find MaKenna right behind him. His hands came out to steady her as she stepped backwards quickly.

"So, now what? Do we rip it out?"

Ciaran nodded. "I would suggest we do. If we do, then I can recess the shelves." He frowned again. "That is, if you're willing to do that."

She nodded. "Just not tonight. Do you want to leave the materials here or take them back to your shop?"

"If I can leave them in the garage, that would work." He reached down to pick up a piece of paper lying near the wall, aged and faded. "Did you see this?" He studied the list of numbers, trying to figure out what they were, flipping it over to see a map. He frowned, thinking he knew where the area was but just not clear on how.

She shook her head. "Frankly, Ciaran. I'm about done in tonight. Take it with you if you want."

He studied it for a moment, a puzzled look on his face. It was a map, but he couldn't think where it was. It looked familiar enough that he knew he wouldn't let it rest until he remembered where.

Chapter 5

A sharp rap on her desk the next morning raised MaKenna's head from her work, and she stared at the man standing there. She pushed back her chair and pointed towards the front of the office.

"You can't be back here. You need to go to the reception area."

He sneered at her. "I'll go wherever I want, little lady. You're not telling me what to do."

She stared at him, taking in the gruff features and unkempt look. She shook her head and moved towards him, forcing him back. "No. You belong out front. Now please move back there."

He reached and grasped her wrist, twisting it as he did so. "Nope. You don't boss me around. Besides, I hear tell you have something I want."

She struggled to release her wrist but couldn't, fear once more rising within her. "Let me go!"

Sudden quick footsteps sounded and her wrist was released. Detective Art Bourne stood there, the man's arm twisted behind his back.

"I've warned you for the last time, Timmy. This time, you're heading for prison."

"What? I wasn't doing anything." The whine grated across MaKenna's nerves.

"No? Then, why are you back here?" He shoved the man towards a patrol officer standing behind him.

MaKenna stepped back from the men, her hand to her mouth, visibly working to control her emotions. Flashes of memory flickered through her mind and her eyes slid closed. She jumped as she felt a hand on her arm, drawing her away from the area and into their small lunch room.

"MaKenna?" Anna's voice reached through the darkness and the voice in her head and MaKenna's eyes opened. "MaKenna? Are you okay?"

MaKenna nodded. "I will be. Just, please, give me a moment." She leaned against the counter in the lunch room, her arms folded across her abdomen, her eyes fastened on the wall in front of her. "Is he gone?"

"He is." The detective's voice was unexpected, and MaKenna jumped even as she turned to face him. "What was that about?"

"I have no idea. I've never seen him before." Her voice died away as she sifted through her memories and thoughts. "No, I'm sure I haven't seen him before."

The detective nodded, even as he shot a look behind him. "We've arrested him for trespassing and assault. He'll be going away for a while. We will need you to come downtown to make a statement."

MaKenna nodded. "But he's not why you were here." She looked past him, hearing voices from the reception area. "Anna, I think you need to be up front. I can hear patients. Let them know the locum is starting next week, or should be, and we'll be in touch with them to book appointments after we've got his schedule." She watched as Anna nodded and moved away.

The detective's keen gray eyes studied MaKenna, noting her distress. "Now, tell me what just happened?"

She shrugged. "He was just there. I don't know how he got past Anna. She was at the reception desk and no one gets by her." She turned to stare at the back door. "Unless he came in that way."

He walked back to look at the door, opening and closing it. "It's not locked. Is it usually?"

MaKenna nodded. "We keep it locked at all times. Now, how did it get unlocked?"

Art Bourne studied her again and then sighed. Whatever was going on with MaKenna, she wasn't about to share with him, and his experience led him to believe something was there, other than why he had met her.

"MaKenna, I just needed to go over the break-in at your home. Just a follow-up. Nothing was taken?"

She shook her head. "No, nothing. I just can't figure out why they tore out the shelving. It's a solid wall there as far as I know."

He nodded and turned, saying over his shoulder, "If you do find something missing or think of anything else, call me."

"I will. Thank you."

MaKenna returned to her desk and picked up her pen, trying to concentrate on the forms she had been working on. She finally threw down her pen and buried her head in her hands. Anna found her that way a short while later.

"MaKenna? What was that all about?"

MaKenna looked up. "To tell you the truth, Anna, I have absolutely no idea. I've never seen him before."

"Then, why were the police here?"

"I had a break-in at home last week. He was just following up on that. And, no. I don't want to talk about it." MaKenna rose, taking a look at the clock. "It's time we're out of here. Have a good night, Anna. I'll lock up."

Anna watched her for a moment before she shrugged and headed for the door, grabbing her purse on the way by. MaKenna watched her leave, a thought crossing her mind before she shook her head and left herself.

Ciaran lifted his tool boxes and headed for MaKenna's door on Saturday morning. She was home, he knew. He could hear Emma barking in the backyard. He tapped at the door, opening it as he heard MaKenna's come in called from somewhere inside the house. He stood for a moment, staring around the living room. What had she done?

MaKenna stood for a moment in the kitchen doorway, watching Ciaran. She was beginning to value his friendship, but held back, not quite sure she could trust him. Trust any man at this point, she decided.

"What did you do, MaKenna?"

She looked around at the gutted living room. "I cleared out what I could, just to make it easier for you. Wasn't I supposed to?" The hesitation in her voice caught at him.

"No, that's great. I just wasn't expecting it. Tell me you didn't lift anything heavy."

She shook her head, before moving towards him. "Where do we start?"

"We?"

She nodded. "We. I want to help."

He shook his head. "Not happening. I don't know what's behind that wall, so I want you to stay back and stay safe."

He walked towards the wall, a frown on his face. "Did you ever track down anyone who knew the home owners?"

"No. I haven't had a chance. Things haven't been going well lately and I've just wanted to hide here with Emma." Her voice sounded lost and alone.

Ciaran spun, staring at her. She had her back to him as she stood in front of the window, not seeing the concern on his face. He shrugged, not wanting to push.

"Okay. We can work on that later. Just let me get started. First, though, where's Emma?"

"She's in the backyard. It's best that she's there. I don't want her spooked."

He nodded even as he reached for his utility knife and made the first cut into the wall. Thirty minutes later, he stood, once more staring at the section of wall. He had been right. The wall was too deep for normal. Puzzled, he stared at the other half of the wall, a distinct feeling of dread coming over him. Something was behind that portion, his gut was telling him, and he had learned to go with his gut.

MaKenna stood beside him, her head tilted.

"Okay. So it is deeper than it should be. That's good, right? That way we can build the bookcases into the wall?"

He nodded, reaching into the cavity. "We can. This looks like the original inside wall. But why would someone put in a fake wall?"

She shrugged. "I have no idea. Whatever they were trying to hide wasn't behind this part." She shuddered, and he shot her a questioning look. "Sorry. It's just with everything that's been going on, I don't feel good about this part."

He nodded, once more reaching to score the drywall with the knife. "Just stand back, then, so I can get to work."

She nodded, reaching to start cleaning up the mess he had made. "Did you say just to drop this on the tarp in the driveway?"

He nodded even as he continued to work. "Please. I'll drop it into the truck and haul it away."

Catching at the drywall with his pry bar, Ciaran pulled, surprised that this section was harder to remove. He finally got a portion away and peeked inside, his hand reaching for a flashlight. He froze as he did so, moving back away from the wall, his face white, the flashlight dropping from his hand.

"Ciaran?" MaKenna's voice spoke behind. "Ciaran? What happened? Why aren't you working on the wall?"

He spun, his hands coming out to stop her from moving towards the wall. "We need to call the police, MaKenna."

"The police? Why? I don't think we need their approval to tear down a wall, do we?"

He nodded as he continued to walk her backwards and outside. "We do, if there's a body behind the wall."

She stared at him, not quite hearing what he was saying. Then her face whitened, and he gripped his hands tighter on her upper arms to hold her upright. "A body? Like in dead? Behind the wall?"

He nodded. "Just like that." He reached to gently shove her into one of the brown wicker chairs on her front porch, then reached for his phone. "Just like that. What other secrets are hiding in here, MaKenna?"

She shivered, not from cold, but from fright. "Is this what it's been about, then?"

Detective Bourne stood in the living room a couple of hours later, watching as the crime scene team carefully helped the coroner move the bones into a body bag. He knew it would be a while yet before he'd have answers, but it was frustrating. He felt that MaKenna was hiding something from him already and now this. He turned and walked out the door, looking for her, and not finding her. He sighed and walked around, through the gate and to the backyard.

Ciaran and MaKenna were seated on the love seat on her back deck. She had her arms wrapped around her upraised legs and her chin on her knees. She watched as he walked towards them and sat heavily into a chair.

"Detective Bourne. Shouldn't we stop meeting this way?"

He shook his head as he gave a half-smile. "I would think so, MaKenna. Do things like this always happen to you?"

She shook her head. "Never in my life. I've been the good girl, always did what I was told, never rebelled. At least until I moved here. For the most part." Her voice died away, and both men felt she hadn't shared something very important with them.

"Rebelled, did you?" He nodded, his eyes on her face, watching for what he wasn't sure. "Talk to me about what happened in there."

She shrugged. "I had no idea that's what we'd find. Ciaran offered to rebuild the shelves, noticed the wall was wider that it should be and started tearing it out." She turned to look at Ciaran, finding his eyes on her. "That's about it."

Ciaran watched as the detective continued to question MaKenna, listening to her quiet responses, sensing the frustration growing in her, and then questioned him. Lord, he prayed, calm her spirit. Reach out to her now.

MaKenna jumped as Ciaran's hand grasped hers, and then she clutched it. The detective watched, sighing to himself. These two are attracted to one another, just what I need.

He pocketed his notepad and stood. "It will be a few hours before they're finished in there. You'll not likely be able to stay here tonight. Do you have somewhere you can go?"

She shrugged. "I'll find somewhere. I won't leave Emma." She peeked down at the dog lying close to her feet. "Thank you, Detective."

Ciaran rose and walked out with Art.

"How safe is she really?" Ciaran's quiet question broke through Art's train of thought.

"I don't know, to tell you the truth. First here at her home and then at work."

"Whoa! Wait a moment!" Ciaran's hands started to wave. "Just what do you mean? At work?"

"She didn't tell you? She had someone approach her at work and rough her up at bit. I happened to be there to follow up her statement."

Ciaran ran his hands through his hair and then clasped them on top of his head. "She never said a word, other than it had been a rough week."

Art nodded. "She's a quiet one. Keeps a lot to herself. The patients all love her though, the ones who approached me. They tell me she's the best one in the office."

Ciaran nodded, then watched the detective drive away before turning to watch the activity going on inside the house. He sighed, walking back around to find

MaKenna. How would he convince her to go stay with his parents or even Beth?

Chapter 6

Sunday morning found Ciaran and Beth seated in their usual seats at the back of the church. He watched for MaKenna, but didn't see her. She had stayed with Beth the previous night but had walked out earlier with Emma, heading for a park.

"Was MaKenna coming today?"

Beth shrugged. "She didn't say this morning. I don't think she slept all that well, from how she looked this morning. I told her not to push it." She looked around. "Oh, there she is. Go get her, Ciaran."

Ciaran's head shot around and he saw MaKenna standing by herself, just inside the door, posed as if to flee. He rose and walked towards her, seeing the relief flit across her face as she saw him.

"MaKenna, you okay?" He stopped in front of her, ducking his head to study her face.

"I am, but I'm not sure I should even be here."

He reached for her hand, raising his face upwards for a moment as his lips compressed. What was going on this morning, Lord? What had brought this on?

"You're where you should be, MaKenna. Come on. Beth has saved us a seat."

Soon seated between the siblings, MaKenna moved restlessly, still not sure she was in the right place. She desperately wanted to talk with Riordan, but knew it wasn't possible. She sighed to herself, not seeing the looks Ciaran and Beth were sharing. She jumped as Ciaran's hand grasped hers and she looked up at him, seeing a look on his face she couldn't understand. Neither of them saw the man walk into the church and sit across the aisle from them, where he could keep an eye on them.

There they were, he thought. Right out in the open. He needed to get whatever it was they had found in that little box. He hadn't planned on them finding that skeleton. He had heard through the grapevine that it had been found. Why couldn't they have let dead bodies lie?

MaKenna's eyes fastened on the minister, Peter Thompson, as he approached the pulpit. She knew somehow that his message this morning would reach her.

She stared at the Bible in her hands, reading over and over the passage he had chosen, not listening to his words at all. She read the verse from Psalm 61, about how the name of the Lord was a strong tower, that she could run to it and be safe. She sighed. If only that was true, she thought. I need that strong tower. Then she caught at the words of the minister as he described building a tower brick by brick, block by block, with few entry points. A sense of peace flooded over her. Is this why I came today, Lord?

Ciaran shifted uncomfortably, feeling eyes on him, eyes that didn't mean friendship. He didn't see anyone overtly watching him, but the presence was there. A presence of evil, he thought. But who was it?

The man followed them from the church and watched as Beth waved and left the two standing there. He could see a discussion going on before they both moved to their vehicles, following one another out of the parking lot.

MaKenna shook her head. Now why had she just agreed to lunch with Ciaran? He had told her to go change from her skirt and sweater into something more casual. He himself was in jeans and a T-shirt.

Ciaran leaned against his truck, watching for MaKenna to come from his sister's home. He had told her to bring Emma as well. He planned on a picnic near the beach and hoped that MaKenna would be agreeable. He straightened as he saw her walking towards him, dressed in faded jeans and a soft sweater.

"You didn't bring Emma?"

She shook her head. "No. It's going to be a hot day and I'd rather she stay somewhere cool."

He nodded, not having realized the effect the heat would have on the dog. "Okay. Now. Let's get you seated and we'll be off."

"And just where does off to mean?"

He laughed as he slid behind the wheel. "A picnic lunch, if that suits my lady."

She stared at him, not quite sure of what he had said. "It suits me fine. You're in a strange mood today."

He just shook his head. "Nope, just being me."

He didn't see the SUV that pulled out from the curb and followed him. His eyes were shifting between the road and the lady sitting beside him. Something had happened in church, he realized.

"Ready to tell me what happened at work last week?"

She shot him a look and then stared out the side window. "Who told you? The detective, I suppose. I had a confrontation with someone and Art was there. I have no idea who he was or what he wanted." She paused, her thoughts running back to the man's words. "He said I had something he wanted. But what?"

"The key? Maybe that's it."

She shrugged. "I have no idea. I have that locked away with all the papers." She turned to stare at him. "You know, sooner or later, we're going to have to go through all those papers." She sighed again as her phone chimed.

"Go ahead. Answer it." Ciaran watched as she pulled it from her pocket and checked the name.

"No. It's just my brother. I'll call him later. We usually talk on Sundays at some point. Although he doesn't usually call this early."

"Call him back then. I don't mind."

"But I do. I don't do this to people I'm with." She watched as a text message appeared on her screen. "Now, what does he mean?"

"What did it say?"

"Just a warning to be very careful and that he needed to talk to me at some point today." She looked up and stared through the windshield. "I never know with Riordan how serious he is. He's always saying stuff like this."

"Crying wolf?"

She nodded. "He does. That's part of the reason I wanted to move away from him and live on my own terms. He's too much a big brother since….." Her voice died away.

"Since?" Ciaran raised an eyebrow at her.

"Nothing."

"One of these days you'll tell me. Now, how about here for our picnic?" He pulled into the parking lot near the beach.

"Oh, this is wonderful. So peaceful."

Hours later, her hand in his, Ciaran led MaKenna back to his truck. Both were sunburned and tired, their feet covered in sand, but happy. They had spread a blanket out under the trees for their lunch of sandwiches and fruit, walked and ran along the shoreline, played in the waves, and just gotten to know one another on a different level. Ciaran knew he wanted to get to know this lady better, that he wanted her to be part of his life. Just how, he wasn't sure.

MaKenna stole a look at Ciaran as he shut the door after her, watching as he rounded the front of the truck and slid behind the wheel. What was it about him that made her feel safe but even more so made her feel cherished?

They didn't see the SUV still sitting where it had been parked, nor the man standing leaning against it. He had been there all afternoon, watching them, waiting for an opportunity that never arose.

Late that evening, Ciaran reached for his phone, seeing it was Beth. He had already retired, knowing that the morning would be an early one. He had to meet a new client before he started work.

"Beth? It's late."

"I know. Ciaran, what did you just say to her?" Her voice accused hm.

"What? Say to who? I haven't talked to anyone."

"You must have. MaKenna has locked herself in her bedroom with Emma and won't talk to me. I can hear her crying. What did you say?"

Ciaran pushed himself up on his pillows. "It wasn't me, Beth. I haven't spoken to her since I dropped her off. Did she get a call?"

"She did. She spoke to whoever it was for about twenty minutes, then brushed by me to go to the bedroom. She was crying, Ciaran." He could hear tears in Beth's voice.

"Let me try and call her. Other than that, just let her have her privacy tonight. If she wants to talk, she will." He thought a moment. "Was it her brother? He tried to reach her earlier today and she didn't take his call."

"No, she spoke with him around suppertime, unless he called back." Beth stood for a moment staring at the closed bedroom door. "I'm scared, Ciaran. I don't like this. I'm not getting a good feeling."

"Let me try and reach her. Talk to her in the morning, hon. Maybe she'll have calmed down enough to tell you."

Beth snorted. "Not likely, Ciaran. That's not MaKenna. She holds things inside."

Ciaran stared at his phone for a moment after he finished his call with his sister, his heart raised in prayer. How did he reach MaKenna? He dialled her number, listening as it went to voice mail. He left a brief message for her.

Not satisfied with that, he sent of a text, asking if she was okay and thanking her for spending the day with him. His finger hesitated over the heart symbol and then thought better of it.

He set his phone down on the night table and waited. His eyes finally closed and he slept, not realizing that MaKenna had received his messages but had decided that what she faced, she had to do on her own.

Chapter 7

Ciaran stood in his sister's kitchen the next night, staring at her, seeing the tears on her face as well as the distress she was feeling. He looked past her for MaKenna and Emma and didn't see either one.

"Beth? Talk to me?" He drew his sister into a hug.

Beth clung to her brother, trying to control her tears. "She's gone, Ciaran. She was gone when I got up this morning. I thought she had just left early without waking me up. When I checked her bedroom this afternoon, she had taken everything."

Ciaran rested his chin on his sister's head. "Do you have her brother's number? Let me call him. Then, I'll go take a look at her house and see if she's back there." He stepped back for a moment, his hands on his sister's shoulders, and studied the face so much like his own. "We'll find her."

"She's stubborn, Ciaran. She won't thank us for looking for her."

"No, I don't imagine she will. But we'll look for her until we find her. She's running from something. I wish she'd let us in." He groaned as his phone rang. As he pulled it out, he prayed that it wouldn't be more bad news about his job site. He had had enough issues there today. He was surprised to see the detective's name flash across the screen.

"Detective? What can I do for you?"

"Ciaran, I have some information on that skeleton you found. Can you and MaKenna come down town tonight?"

Ciaran hesitated before he spoke. "I can, but I'm not sure about MaKenna."

"MaKenna? Is there a problem there? I tried to reach her and only got her voice mail." He sounded frustrated at that.

"I'm not sure, Art. She left my sister's place early this morning and we don't know exactly where she is." He walked towards his truck. "I'm heading towards her home now."

"Just a moment. You're sure about that?" Ciaran could hear voices in the background. "Ciaran, she didn't show up for work today. Was there a problem there today?"

"I have no idea." Ciaran had put his phone on handsfree as he drove across town, his eyes watchful, his head turning as he drove, searching for MaKenna, Emma, or her car. "I had talked to her since around suppertime last night. I spent the afternoon with her and everything was fine when I dropped her off at my sister's. Other than her brother had tried to get ahold of her and she mentioned that he had warned her to be careful."

"Do you have his number?"

"No, I don't. He's a pastor in a town two hours from here. His first name's Riordan. That's all she's said."

He could hear the detective muttering to himself before he spoke. "Okay, I'll try and track him down. If you speak to either her brother or MaKenna, I do need to talk to both of you. Tonight, preferably."

"I can come in, but I'm at MaKenna's now." He parked and turned off the truck, his eyes searching the building and surrounding area. "Let me see if she's here. I'll call you back." He hung up on the detective's words, not catching his warning.

Ciaran stood for a moment, his eyes searching the area, a frown on his face. He didn't like the vibes he was getting, or the fact that he felt watched. Not at all. Where are you, MaKenna? He didn't hear Emma barking. Knocking at the door and ringing the doorbell didn't work. He peeked through the window and didn't see MaKenna. Sighing to himself, he walked around to the backyard, praying she was there. He could see evidence that she had been that day: a mug on the table, an empty chocolate bar wrapper, some dog cookies. Looking down, he saw the fresh water in the bowl for Emma.

Where are you, MaKenna? What has happened to you? He spun in a circle, eyes searching for her. He turned as he heard the door open behind him and stared at her. She looked frustrated, exhausted, and worried as she stared at him, a perplexed look on her face.

MaKenna shook her head. "Ciaran, what are you doing here?"

"Looking for a friend?" He stepped towards her, his eyes watchful, his heart sinking at he took her the shuttered look on her face and in her eyes.

"Go away." She started to close the door but stopped as he spoke.

"MaKenna, I have no idea what happened or why you left so early this morning. Beth is beside herself with worry. I've had the detective call me. He needs to speak with us."

She stared at him for a moment, before she stepped back. "Come in, then, and I'll grab my purse." She didn't sound very welcoming.

He shook his head. "I'll be around front." He frowned as he walked back to the front of the house to wait for her. He hadn't heard Emma or seen her when MaKenna had opened the door.

MaKenna stared down at Emma as she stood inside the door, her hand on the lock. She didn't like leaving Emma on her own, not after the scare she had had last night. Someone had threatened Emma, and she knew she had to protect her somehow, but just how, she wasn't sure. All she knew was that she had to withdraw from her friends until she figured out exactly what was going on. She had secrets in her past, secrets that Riordan was after her to share, and she just wasn't ready to do that. She didn't know if she would ever be. She bent to hug her dog and drop a kiss on the silky head before stepping outside and locking up.

"Where's Emma?" Ciaran's words startled her enough for her to drop her keys. He reached for them, his fingers brushing hers as he handed them back. "Do you want to take her with you?"

She stared at him for a moment, then turned back to the door. "I'll be a moment." She locked the door as she let Emma out on her leash. She was still hesitant about taking her. "But what do I do with her while we're talking with the detective?"

"She goes in with us. I'm pretty sure it will be okay. If not, then he can meet us outside." Ciaran was adamant that neither MaKenna or Emma would be left on their own.

MaKenna kept her arms tight around Emma as she watched through the truck window, her eyes alert to anything that might alarm her. She hadn't heard from that man again today, but she knew he was watching her. The pictures he had sent last night showed that.

Ciaran stood at the counter in the police station, MaKenna's hand tight in his. She had Emma's leash gripped tight in her other hand, not wanting to risk losing her. He studied her face, seeing the dark shadows under her eyes, the paleness of her skin, the hollow spots in her cheeks, the fatigue in just the way she moved and breathed. He needed to end this for her but had no idea how to do just that or even who it was. He turned as he heard footsteps heading his way.

Art stood for a moment, assessing the couple in front of him, and yes, he acknowledged to himself, they were a couple. He frowned a bit when he saw Emma until he saw the desperation in MaKenna's face and the determination in Ciaran's.   Yes, he thought, they won't let Emma out of their sight, neither one of them. He sighed. Now what?

He opened the door to let them in and pointed towards his office. They shook their heads at his offer of something to drink. He felt eyes on him and turned, to find the dog watching him, assessing him, keeping her distance, but vigilant. He shook his head. It was the first time he felt like he had been weighed and found wanting by a dog. He motioned to the chairs by his desk and then seated himself heavily in his own chair, his joints and back aching with the strain of what his day had been, and it didn't look like it would be ending any time soon. He had too many cases to work on and not enough hours in the day.

Ciaran's gaze moved between Art and MaKenna, who were staring at one another. He frowned, not quite sure what was going on

"Art? You asked to see us." Ciaran's questioning voice drew Art's gaze to him.

"I did. I have some things I need to go over with you." He paused, not quite sure how to proceed, his hand reaching for a file folder, before he dropped the folder in front of him. He was suddenly unsure of how to proceed, and that was unlike him. "I found out the name of the man whose skeleton was found in the wall. He was Timothy Wilson. He didn't own the house and wasn't a relative of the family."

"Then, how…." MaKenna's voice dropped away and she paled even more. "Did they say how old they thought he was?"

"In his forties, the coroner said. He couldn't give us a cause of death, but the team is still searching through the debris they picked up there."

"So, it's possible he was killed somewhere else and then put there?" Ciaran was thinking aloud, trying to puzzle it out.

"It's possible. We just don't know. He wasn't a permanent resident of this town, though, so that makes it difficult to trace his movements prior to his death." Art kept his eyes on MaKenna. "He actually came from a town two hours from here."

MaKenna's eyes flew to his, and her face whitened even more as her fingers tightened on the leash she held. "What did you say?"

"I said he came from Maple River. Know that town?" Art was pushing MaKenna and they both knew it. Ciaran's eyes shifted between the two, not quite sure what was going on.

"He's been dead for how long?" MaKenna had to wet her lips in order to speak, her voice low and hoarse.

Art shrugged. "About fifteen years, they think. They can't be quite sure." He dropped his eyes to the file folder before pulling out a photo and sliding it across the desk towards her. "Here. This is what he looked like. Do either of you recognize him?"

Ciaran studied the photo, from a driver's license he thought, taking in the thin gray hair, beard and stocky build of the man. "No, I don't. MaKenna?"

He turned and was in time to catch her as she slid from the chair, Emma on her feet pushing towards her mistress. Art pointed at the couch behind the chairs, and Ciaran moved quickly that way, laying MaKenna down. Art reached for a bottle of water and handed it to Ciaran, who pulled out a handkerchief and moistened it, using it to wipe across MaKenna's face.

"What just happened?" Anger roughened Ciaran's voice, and he turned to glare at the detective.

"Not what I expected, that's for sure. I wonder…". He turned and headed back to his desk, picking up the folder and leafing it through it once more. Then, he groaned. "I didn't make the connection before. This is her mother's brother."

"Her uncle? Then how did he got into that wall?" Ciaran stared at him, shock on his face, before he turned to stare at MaKenna again. "What is going on?"

MaKenna stirred, her eyes flickering open to stare up at Ciaran, before they slid closed again as she gave a soft sigh. Ciaran touched her face, calling her name, with no effect. He spun on his knees from where he knelt beside the couch and stared up at Art.

Art pocketed his phone. "I just called for the EMS. They'll take her to the hospital." He stared down at Emma who had jumped up with her mistress and even now lay covering her legs. "What do we do with her dog?"

Ciaran pulled out his phone. "I'll call my sister. She'll take her." He pocketed his phone once he had done so and reached for MaKenna's hand, trying to warm the chilled fingers.

Art stepped to the side as he watched the paramedics work on MaKenna, who hadn't regained consciousness. He turned as he heard Ciaran greeting someone and realized he knew Beth after all from a Bible study they both belonged to. He nodded a greeting as she reached for Emma's leash and let the reluctant Sheltie from the room, Emma's head turning to watch MaKenna until she was taken out of sight. Art shook his head. He just didn't get it, how the dog wouldn't leave MaKenna.

Ciaran watched as well, his eyes not leaving MaKenna's still form. He moved back as the paramedics wheeled the stretcher from the room, then headed after them to find his truck, not stopping to speak with Art at all, his mind solely on the lady ahead of him. Art watched, then shook his head, a small smile on his face. He would have to catch up with the two later. He frowned, his eyes going back to the folder as he picked it up. He studied it once more, then reaching for the phone, dialled a number and spoke to the detective in the other town.

MaKenna stirred, her eyes flickering open and closed as she roused. They finally stayed open, and she frowned as she stared around. This wasn't her bedroom. Why was she in a hospital room? Movement and a slight noise to her left caused her to jump and her eyes flew that way, fright in them. She relaxed as she saw her brother, Riordan, standing there.

"Hey, sis. About time you woke up." Riordan leaned over the bed rail to drop a kiss on her head.

"What are you doing here?" Her voice was raspy, and he reached for the glass of water to help her drink.

"I heard you needed someone to look after you." He frowned, a puzzled look in his eyes. "I got your message from last night. I just didn't expect to see you in the hospital."

She shrugged, her hands working on the blanket. "I didn't expect to be here either. Are you alone?"

He nodded. "I didn't let Mom and Dad know. And that friend of yours? The one who wouldn't leave? Who challenged me? He finally left to go to work."

"What time is it?" Her eyes slid closed even as she asked. The fatigue was weighing the lids down and she fought against.

"It's about 9 a.m. What happened to you?" Riordan's voice was stern, the one he used to use when they were kids and he wanted to make her do what he said.

She peeked at him through partially open eyelids. "Did you talk to anyone here?" When he shook his head, she continued. "I got another one of those calls Sunday night, you know. The one where no one talks but I get all these texts messages after I answer with all those pictures? Then, I told you about the skeleton, didn't I?"

"Skeleton? What skeleton? Just what aren't you telling me?" Riordan stared at his sister, his mind racing as to what she really meant. He narrowed his eyes as he once more took in the fatigue that she was feeling. "Talk to me, MaKenna. Tell me what is going on with you."

"First, why did you call me like that on Sunday?" She peered at him through half-open eyes.

"What do you mean?" He slid a chair over, seated himself and then lowered the bedrail so he could see her properly.

"You sent me a text message to be careful?"

He finally nodded. "I did. I have no idea why I did. Just a real sense of danger I had about you. Looks as if I was right, though, doesn't it?"

She sighed, her eyes going to the door. "Is there anyone out there?"

"Like the cop at the door?" He gave a grim smile as her eyes shot to his.

"No, don't tell me he did that." She groaned and her head went back on the pillow. She reached for the control and raised the head of the bed, wincing at the headache that came with the movement.

"Hey, take it easy there. What all aren't you telling me? Why is there a cop at the door?"

"I have no idea. I can remember talking to Ciaran and the detective last night. Next thing, I know, I'm here and so are you." She wouldn't look at her brother, her eyes on her fingers picking at the blanket.

"Does this have anything to do with why you left town, moved here?" Riordan waited, not quite sure how to ask what he needed to ask.

She shook her head. "No. I just needed to get away from Mom and Dad. I felt like I didn't have a life. I needed to be somewhere I had to rely on myself, not them." She looked at her brother, tears shimmering in her eyes. "Do you understand?"

"I do, MaKenna, but I'm not sure they do. Dad is determined to bring you back home, and if he finds out about this, you won't be able to stop him."

She shook her head vehemently. "That's not happening. He means well, but I am an adult and need to stand on my own two feet. Although I'm not sure if work is still going to be there."

Riordan waited patiently, knowing she'd tell him when she was ready. She finally sighed, her eyes sliding closed as she spoke, telling him exactly why she had left their hometown, what had happened at her work, and what had happened in her home, ending with the text messages she was receiving again.

He sat back, not realizing what all she had been going through. He had known of some of the text messages she had received, but not that they had started up again. Lord, how do I reach her? She's hurting, hiding, and not trusting You as she should. What is the purpose in all this? I know You have a plan and purpose for all this but I just don't see it and I know MaKenna doesn't either.

Chapter 8

Riordan helped his sister into her house, looking first for Emma before realizing that she was still with Beth. He would need to go get her, he thought. They needed each other. He watched as MaKenna sank down on her couch, her face whitening as she stared at the bare wall and its memories.

"Do you want to sit somewhere else?" Riordan sat beside her, his shoulder touching hers, trying to bring her comfort.

She shook her head. "No. It's okay. It's just that I don't know if I'll be able to live here again, knowing that our uncle was barricaded behind those walls." She blinked back tears before she looked at him. "Don't you have to be home tonight?"

He shook his head. "I talked to the church board chair and asked for a couple of days off. He told me to be back for Bible study and prayer on Wednesday night, but if you really needed me, just to let him know. So, I can stay until tomorrow afternoon."

"Thank you, Riordan. I need you here for the next couple of days." She hugged him, then stood on shaky legs before making her way to the kitchen. "I need some tea. Which do you prefer, tea or coffee?"

"Tea's good." He stood, leaning against the kitchen doorjamb, one leg crossed over the other, arms folded across his chest, assessing how she was doing. "Just how are you, now that you're home?"

She shrugged, even as she worked around the counter, plugging in the kettle, reaching for the teapot and filling the tea ball with the loose tea leaves.

She finally set their mugs on the table and turned to the fridge. "Are you hungry?"

Riordan moved towards her, pulling her into a hug. "MaKenna, I know what you're doing. You can't hide. Activity is not going to make this go away. We need to talk about it and make plans."

She shook her head even as she returned his hug. He gave the best brother hugs, she thought. "I'm just so confused right now, Riordan. Who is doing this? Why? How did Uncle Timothy die and get buried here? And how did I end up buying this very house?"

He looked down at her, before pushing her into her chair. "Sit. Let's pray first okay?" He sighed as his phone rang. "That's Dad. What do I tell him?"

Her eyes shot to his and she began to shake her head. "Nothing. I don't want him here."

He tilted his head to study her. "What happened to you two after I left for seminary?"

She shook her head again. "Nothing that I could put my finger on. It's just that once you were gone, I didn't have my buffer any more, and he began to be very demanding of what he thought I should do. He was smothering me, chasing away my friends. It took a while for me to get up the courage to break away. He didn't want me to even go to college."

Riordan sat back, not having realized how hard his little sister had had it after he left. "I never knew, sis. I wish I had. Please, never hide anything from me again."

She nodded, then stared at the doorway as the doorbell rang. She sighed, rising to her feet. "Thank you, Riordan."

He rose and followed her, standing back as she peeked out and then opened the door.

"Detective, what can I do for you? Come in. I think you've met my brother, Riordan."

"Thank you, MaKenna. I have met him, yes." His keen eyes studied her, then lifted to catch the protective look on Riordan's face. "I just needed to talk to you again. Can we sit somewhere?"

"We're in the kitchen. Do you drink tea? Because that's all that's ready right now." Riordan choked back a laugh at her words, causing the detective to frown at him.

Art studied the siblings, seeing the likeness and the differences between the two, before he spoke.

"Are you feeling better?"

She shrugged. "I have no idea. There's just been too much going on lately for me to really know. Now, you said you wanted to talk to me. About what?"

Art smiled, not shocked at her words. "I did. About last night. I'm sorry if the shock was too much. I didn't realize the connection when I showed you the photo."

He studied his hands for a moment. "Do you know anything about your uncle?"

The two siblings shared a glance before MaKenna spoke. "Mom never talked about him much. I sort of remember him, but not really. I just recognized the picture."

Riordan agreed. "He was a closed subject, that's for sure. I don't think Mom mentioned him more than a dozen times. She never said why."

Art nodded. "I would be interested in talking with your mother, to see what light she can shed on this. We had a missing person's report on him but it went cold years ago. We've now reopened that cold case." He paused, not quite sure how to continue. "The crime scene team did find a knife in what they gathered here."

"Any evidence as to if he was killed here or brought here?"

Art shook his head at Riordan's question. "That we can't answer. And we're trying to retrace the steps of someone who didn't want to be followed. That's very difficult at any time but after all this time?"

MaKenna rose as the doorbell rang again, muttering under her breath. Riordan smothered his grin, knowing it would bring her wrath down on him if she saw it. The two men listened to the words at the front door before Art rose and headed that way.

MaKenna stood in her doorway, fear evident in her stance. Art stopped behind her, his eyes on the woman standing there. He studied her enough to memorize the gray hair, hard brown eyes, and hatred on her face.

"Ma'am? Can I help you?" He pulled out his badge and gently moved MaKenna behind him.

The woman glared at him, then past him at MaKenna. "I want in this house. It belonged to my brother."

"I'm sorry, but if the homeowner says no, then that's it."

She snorted. "She doesn't own this house."

"Sorry, but I have the paperwork and everything I need to prove it. Are you calling me a thief in front of a police officer? Because if you are, then you need to prove it or face arrest." MaKenna moved back in front of Art to confront the woman.

The woman stared at her in hatred, then turning, stomped down the sidewalk to her car. Art caught the plate number and moved away to make a call. Riordan had risen and come out at the angry words, finally drawing his sister back into the house.

"Who else are you expecting today, sis?" His gentle teasing calmed her down and she finally smiled.

"I would expect Beth with Emma and I'm sure Ciaran will be along. I hope that's all. I can't take many more." She stood, her hands rubbing up and down her arms, shutting down on them.

Art studied her for a moment, then with a quiet word to Riordan, walked away. He had an investigation to run and it didn't seem as if MaKenna would be of help to him that day.

Late that night, Ciaran sat on his back deck, a cup of coffee beside him, the only light coming from the solar lights set around the deck and yard. He had turned off the lights in the house and relished the darkness of the night. It was not often that he had an opportunity just to sit and ponder on God's word and ways. He had been reading in Psalm 61, thinking about the stronghold that God had provided, and knowing somehow that both he and MaKenna would have need of it and soon.

He heard a whisper of sound and spun in his chair, trying to make out who was there in the darkness, and not seeing anyone. He rose and walked down the steps to the grass and then turned in a circle once more. Someone was there, he was sure, but just who or why he didn't know.

Sudden movement to his left had him turning that way before he was tackled and sent to the ground, the bone-jarring landing reverberating through his body. He groaned, then struggled to rise, his face buried in the grass. The heavy weight on his back didn't move, and he felt an arm shoved against his neck and then the prick of a knife near his ear. He froze. The arm shoved harder against his neck, and then he heard a guttural voice.

"Where is it? We know you have it. If you want to live, turn it over. You wouldn't want anything nasty to happen to your pretty lady, now would you?"

Ciaran tried to shake his head, to rise, to throw off the weight on his back, but couldn't. Lord, help me.

"I don't know what you want. How can I help you if I don't?"

"It wasn't in the box. Now, where is it?"

"Where's what? I don't know what it is." Ciaran repeated himself even as he remembered. It had to be the key. But what did that key even open?

"We'll be back. Make sure you have what we want. Remember. Our eyes are on you and your lady. It would be a real shame if something nasty happened to her, now wouldn't it, just because you didn't cooperate." With a final shove at Ciaran's neck, the man rose and was gone, light on his feet for his size.

Ciaran lay there on the grass, arms outstretched, as he tried to regain his breath and recover. He rose slowly, his hand rubbing at his neck and then fingering the small cut below his ear. The man was serious, he thought. I need to protect MaKenna, but I don't know how to. She's shutting down, Lord, and I can't reach her at all. And what does that key open, anyway, and how does it coordinate with the death of Timothy Wilson? His brain refused to think and he sighed, knowing he had to leave his thoughts until the next day. But he would be seeing MaKenna, that was a given.

The next morning, MaKenna stood in her office at work, looking around. The locum doctor was starting on Monday, and she needed to be ready for that. Anna wasn't in, and that was unlike her. She had talked with her the previous evening and Anna had been eager to be there, to help get things ready for the new doctor.

MaKenna sighed and turned to lock the outside door, stopping to pick up the mail as she walked by Anna's desk. She knew there would be many messages on the voice mail, and they needed to be dealt with first.

Two hours later, she finally reached for the mail again, quickly sorting it. Lab reports, she thought, I need to pull the charts, and stood. Something was different in her office and she wasn't quite sure what. She shrugged, heading for the file room with the reports in her hand. Stacking the charts on the desk in the doctor's office, she turned in a circle again, feeling eyes on her but she was alone and the blinds were closed. So, how did she have that feeling? She shrugged and walked back to her desk to deal with the rest of the mail.

A plain white envelope with just her name on it was sitting on her desk. It hadn't been there before, she was sure of that. So, where did it come from? She froze, her eyes searching the room around her, panic rising. Had he found her again? She almost ran for the reception area, her hand fumbling to pull her phone from her pocket, even as she checked that the door was still locked. The phone shook as she dialled Art's number, reaching his voice mail. She left a message, then sank to the floor in a corner of the room, her head buried against her knees, her arms wrapped tight around her legs. He had been in here, while she was by herself. How did he get in again through a locked door?

Art stood staring down at the envelope before he reached into his pocket for a pair of latex gloves. He had received MaKenna's voice mail about ten minutes after she left it, and the panic in her voice had sent him her way in a hurry. He didn't like this, not one bit. How many people were involved with this? And how many more events would be entwined before he had it all sorted out?

"You didn't touch it?" He raised his eyes to MaKenna, who stood in the doorway, visibly shaking. "Walk me back through what you did once you got here."

She did just that, but stopped. "When I put the reports on the desk in the doctor's office, I felt like I was being watched. But how could I be when I locked the door and was sure I was the only one here. It was right after I felt like I was being watched that I found that." Her finger stabbed at the envelope he held.

"I have no idea, MaKenna, but I think it's a good idea of the locks are changed. You say Anna wasn't in and never called?"

She shook her head. "No, and that's not like her."

"Do you have her address? I can send someone to check on her."

She nodded and headed back to the reception area, returning with a slip of paper. "Here. This is where she lives."

"Thank you." Art reached for his phone and giving the address, asked for a welfare check. "They'll call and let me know what they've found." He was worried and trying not to let MaKenna know that.

He turned the envelope over in his hands, frowning. He opened the back flap, which had been tucked down into the envelope and pulled out the card inside, his eyes shooting to MaKenna.

"MaKenna, is there something you should be telling me?" His voice, though quiet, had a question more than what he asked.

"What do you mean?" She was puzzled at his words.

"Come here." He waited, then repeated himself. "Take a look at this."

She looked at his face, standing still until he beckoned her forward. She moved slowly towards him, not sure she wanted to see what was in the envelope. He pointed at the desk, waiting for her to react, before raising his eyes to find her still staring at him.

"MaKenna, I need you to look at what's on the desk, not try to see it in my mind." He gave a half-grin as he said that, and she shook her head and looked down.

Her face whitened even more as her hands went to her mouth. She began shaking her head, even as she stepped back until she leaned against the wall.

Art watched her, then turned back to the card. He flipped the card over and froze. A picture of MaKenna and Emma was taped there, taken within the last couple of days, he bet. He turned it back over to read the congratulations on her engagement. Except there was no name, just a question mark.

"Art, please. Make that disappear." MaKenna's finger pointed at the card. "He's back and doing it again."

"Makenna? Who's back and doing what?" He muttered to himself as his phone chimed. "Bourne. Not there? What's that?" He paused as he turned to stare at MaKenna, a frown on his face. "Yeah, have the team go there. And I'll need them at Stirling's office again. Thanks."

He turned to MaKenna. "Now, explain to me what you meant when you said he's back and doing it again."

She shook her head, then nodded. "I have no idea who he is. Not really. I went through this in Maple Grove for about a year. Riordan helped me look for who it was, but we couldn't figure out who it was."

"Did you file a police report?" When she shook her head, he spoke. "You should have. It would show a pattern."

"I couldn't. You don't understand what it's like in that town."

"Then, tell me. Help me to understand." He reached out a hand to draw her back to the reception area as the crime scene techs entered. He pointed to a chair and waited for her to sit. "Now. Talk to me."

She shuddered as the memories returned. "I never knew who it was. I have saved all the texts and voice mails,

94

downloading them to my computer at home. I can give them to you. We can't track his phone. It comes up as an unlisted number." She sat back, her face white and drawn, her eyes haunted. "No one really knows how bad or how many. Not until today and you. I have to stop him, but I don't know how. And I don't know how it involves whatever is going on here." Her hand waved to take in the office area.

"That's good. I can get them from you later. Continue. Tell me why you didn't go to the police in your town."

She shuddered again, her head going back to lean on the wall behind her chair. "It's a small town. Dad was really good friends with the police chief. Any report I filed? He would have been told about it. I would have become a prisoner in my own home, not allowed any freedom at all."

He frowned. "Your father shouldn't have been able to get that kind of information."

She raised her head to stare at him. "That's how that town works, Art. The police tell family members everything about their families. That's part of the reason I moved from there. And if you call and ask for any information, Dad will be here before you could even hang up the phone."

"It's that bad?"

She nodded. "It is." She stared down the hall at the techs before rising. "Do you need anything else from me right now? Because if you don't, I just want to go home and cuddle with my dog."

✯ ✯ ✯ ✯ ✯

Setting aside his Bible with a bookmark in place, Ciaran rose and stretched. It had been a long week, and he looked forward to the weekend. He picked up his phone and frowned. MaKenna was to have called him and hadn't. He peered at the clock. It was still early evening. He reached for his keys, heading for the door, when he stopped, a thought freezing him in place. He turned, his eyes running over the living room furniture until he spotted it. He reached for the folder he had placed on the table after work and then was out the door and into his truck, heading to see her. He smiled, anticipation rising at her reaction to the news he had found.

He tapped at her door, not liking that she hadn't responded. He walked around to the backyard, disappointed that she wasn't there. He stood for a moment, eyes searching

96

the area, looking for anything out of the ordinary before walking to the back gate and opening it. He froze for a moment as he saw the package, then spun to stare at the house again before turning to the package again. What was going on with her?

"Ciaran? What are you doing?" A soft voice behind him caused him to spin.

"MaKenna? Where were you?" He studied her, seeing the dark shadows on her face and the fatigue.

"I had been sleeping." She yawned, her hand going up to cover her mouth. "Emma alerted that someone was out here. When I checked, I saw your truck." She leaned sideways to look around him. "What is that?"

He shrugged as he turned to stare down at it. "I have no idea. Looks like just some garbage."

"You think? Should we open it?"

He shook his head. "No. Can you get me a garbage bag and I'll put it into the trash. There's a lot of garbage blowing around today."

She was back quickly with a bag, watching as he scooped up the package and headed around to his truck. "Come back in when you're done, Ciaran. I need to talk to you."

He stopped, throwing her a look of curiosity and then nodded. Two minutes later, he was seated at her kitchen table, a cup of coffee in hand as she headed to her office. She returned with a pile of papers, some of which he recognized as those he had pulled from the ceiling cavity.

"I've been reading through these and doing some research. This house has a dirty little secret, I think."

"A dirty little secret, does it?" A grin twitched at his lips, and she frowned at him.

"It's not funny, Ciaran."

He held up his hands. "I know it's not." He reached for her hands. "Listen. There is one thing we haven't done yet, with all that's been going on. Come on." He wiggled his fingers at her as he grinned at her. "Just take my hands, already, will you? We need to spend some time in prayer, asking for wisdom, guidance and protection. We haven't done that. I just feel that this is escalating and we need to do this."

She finally grasped his hands, feeling the roughness of his against the smoothness of hers. She liked the feeling of that, and shouldn't, she thought. Once this was over, they'd part ways and she would likely move on to another town, to another job. That depressed her.

Ciaran's voice cut through her thoughts and she listened at the easy conversational tone in his voice as he prayed, wishing she could talk to God that way as well.

"So, what did you find out?" Ciaran reached for the papers she had set down. He sorted through them, scanning each one. He finally paused as one and read it through, then re-read it before lifting his eyes to meet hers.

"MaKenna? What's this?" He tapped the paper with one finger.

"Which one is that?" She reached over and pulled his hand down so she could see which one he was reading. "Oh, that one. I'm still researching that."

"Why? What made you decide to do that?"

She shrugged, her eyes back on the paper she had been reading. "I don't know. Just something I thought I should do. Why?"

"Why? Because I think this is the key, no pun intended." He sorted through the papers again until he found the one he wanted. "This one? It goes with this."

"How'd you figure that out?" She rose to stand behind him, reading over his shoulder, one hand on his shoulder to keep herself balanced.

Ciaran stilled for a moment, liking the feel of her hand on his shoulder, then pointed to the two papers. "See? The names are the same. And here. This lists the relatives." He sat for a moment, then reached for more papers, handing her a stack. "Here, sort them into order by date. There's a pattern here I'm seeing."

"I'm glad someone is. I missed that." She rubbed at her neck, trying to relieve the stress. "Art told me they found Anna. She's not saying why she didn't show up for work. He's under the impression she's scared for her life."

Ciaran nodded as he glanced up, catching a shadow of fear that crossed her face. What was going on here, Lord? Why is she so afraid? Help her to trust You and run to that strong tower.

MaKenna jumped as her phone chimed, not expecting it to. She reached for it, frowning as she saw it was her brother

"Riordan? Why are you calling me tonight? We just spoke this morning." She wasn't happy with her brother and his interruption.

"MaKenna? Are you at home? Are you by yourself?" Riordan's voice was rushed and almost panicked.

"Riordan? What's going on? I'm home, and Ciaran is here. We're working on those papers I showed you." She raised her eyes to Ciaran, who had stopped working and was watching her, a frown on his face. He motioned for her to put the phone on speaker.

"Riordan? Ciaran here. What's wrong?" He reached for MaKenna's hand, sensing she would need the support he could give her.

"MaKenna, you need to get out of the house, now. Pack what you can and go find somewhere safe. Not to Beth's."

"Riordan? You're scaring me. What's going on?"

"It's Dad. He's on his way there. I just found out. He's planning on bringing you back home, one way or another."

"He can't do that. I'm an adult."

"Yeah, I know. But he's trying to work it out to prove that you're unstable and a danger to yourself. Leave now. Pack up what you can. I'm heading for their place. Something's wrong there. I can't get in touch with Mom." His voice faded for a moment, then came back strong. "Don't take your phone. He's put some kind of tracking program on it, so he knows where you are at all times."

Her anger rising, she stood. "Let me know what's up with Mom." She stopped as Ciaran's hand was landed on her arm.

"Riordan. Use my phone number. I'm pulling the SIM card from MaKenna's."

"Do that. Listen, I'm almost at the house. Dad left about ninety minutes ago, so he'll be there in less than an hour." His voice died away as the connection was broken.

Ciaran stood, taking charge as MaKenna just stood. "MaKenna, go. Pack. I'll get Emma's stuff. You want her crate as well?" He spoke again, his voice rough with worry, and watched as she nodded, then spun and ran for her bedroom. He swept the papers and photos into a pile and found a backpack to stuff them in. By the time MaKenna had returned, he had everything loaded in the truck. He watched as she turned off lights, taking one last look at her phone, now turned off, before reaching for her Bible and sticking it into the top of the bag.

Ciaran almost shoved her into his truck and slid behind the wheel, his thoughts on what Riordan had said, his prayers flying skyward. He sped away from MaKenna's home, not sure when she would return there.

"Ciaran, where are you going?"

He shook his head. "I'm not sure, MaKenna. I can't take you to Beth. Your Dad knows where she lives." Then he groaned and reached for his phone, pulling to the side of the road. "Beth? Lock your doors and don't answer them. You may have trouble heading your way." At her cry of surprise, he stopped. "Listen. Riordan just called. Their Dad's on his way to MaKenna's, with plans to force her to go home. Don't let him in. If he shows up, call it in."

He stuffed his phone back into his pocket, pulling away from the curb, his eyes searching for what vehicle he wasn't sure of.

"Ciaran?" MaKenna's voice was soft, but he could hear the fear and worry in it. "Where am I to go? And I know I can't go back to the office. He's been there, and he'll look for me there on Monday, if he can't find me over the weekend."

"I know. I'm trying to think of a place. If he knows Beth, then he'll track me down."

His eyes shifted to the rearview mirror. Was that car following him? No, it turned. He breathed a little easier. Where could he take MaKenna where she could be safe?

"MaKenna, call Art. Let him know what's going on. We may need his help."

Her eyes flew to his face. "No, that's not right. We don't, do we?"

His face was grim as he nodded. "We may well do. Now, call. Let him know what's going on. I suspect he contacted the police there and somehow your father found out."

"I'm sure he did. He has the police in his pocket."

"What?" Ciaran threw her a grim look. "Has that happened in the past?"

She fingered his phone, her eyes down. Emma whined, placing her muzzle on MaKenna's arm. "It's what he always does. He's getting worse, more so since Riordan left home."

"I didn't know that, Makenna. I'm sorry." Ciaran couldn't fathom a family life like that. His family was close, walking in and out each's other lives, but letting them live their own without interference.

MaKenna stuck Ciaran's phone back into the cup holder. "He did call, not realizing what would happen. He has information that he wants to get to us." Her eyes searched the darkening sky. "Ciaran, we've been driving for an hour now. Where are we heading? And it seems you've been driving in circles."

He gave a short laugh. "You're observant finally. I have been. I'm trying to think of where to go." He looked down as his phone chimed. "Check that, will you?"

She read the text. "He found his way to Beth's. She had to call the police because he wouldn't leave." Fear froze her features. "What now, Ciaran? He won't stop until he finds me and drags me home."

"We won't let him." He stopped the truck in a strip mall parking lot and turned it off, shifting in his seat to study her. "Riordan hasn't called. Call him."

She shot him a glance and then dialled her brother. "Riordan? What did you find?"

"He hurt Mom, MaKenna. I'm on the way to the hospital. I'm not sure yet how bad. She told me she tried to stop him from coming after you."

Tears trickled down her cheeks and she swiped angrily at them. "Why, Riordan? Why does he have to be like this?"

"I don't know, sis. Stay safe. I'll call as soon as I have word. And no, I don't think you should come just yet. Let me talk to Ciaran, please."

She handed to the phone to Ciaran, not listening to his side of the conversation, her head on her hand as she stared out the window, wiping at the tears on her face. She jumped when Ciaran touched her hand.

"MaKenna. Let's find somewhere for tonight. I'd take you to Mom but they're away for the weekend."

She nodded, her eyes on his face. "What did Riordan say to you?"

He shook his head. "Not tonight. We need to get you safe. You need to sleep well tonight. It will be soon enough to talk tomorrow."

He drove away from the mall, watching for any vehicle that seemed to be chasing after them, not seeing one. He finally pulled into his driveway and then into his garage. "We should be okay here tonight. He can't get into the house. We'll go in through the garage, and keep the lights off as much as we can."

She nodded, not moving. "Ciaran, I don't like putting you at risk. I can't ask you to do more."

"You didn't ask. I volunteered. Besides, I never turn my back on friends."

She nodded, following him into the house, watching as he let Emma out into the yard before reaching for her bowl and filling it with water.

"I thought you didn't like dogs." She was puzzled. He was opening up in ways she didn't expect, especially where her dog was concerned.

"Emma grows on you, you know. I know you need her with you. But if it comes to it, would you let me take her somewhere she'll be safe until we can solve this?"

She hesitated, her eyes on her dog as she came back into the house, knowing how much she treasured her and relied on her to calm her down. She shrugged, not willing to put into words her feelings. He nodded, then pointed towards the hall, showing her the guest room.

"It has an attached bath. I remodelled this home when I bought it. If you need anything, I'll be in the living room."

"You need to sleep too, Ciaran."

He smiled as his hand reached to caress her cheek. "I will, sweetheart, but I'll feel better if I do that in the living room."

He watched as she shut the door, closing herself and Emma in for the night, before he paced the living room, his thoughts on what Riordan had asked of him. He finally sat, his head in his hands, his thoughts on the lady down the hall. He finally dropped to his knees, ready to spend the night in prayer, seeking to find out what his Father would have him do.

Chapter 9

Ciaran waited for MaKenna to appear the next morning. He reached to make a cup of tea for her, knowing that's what she prefer, and refilled his coffee cup. He scrubbed his hands down his face, feeling the growth of whiskers, and sighed. He needed to shower and shave. He glanced at the clock and groaned. It was still really early. Why did he expect MaKenna to be up at six o'clock in the morning? Even on weekends, he couldn't sleep in. Getting up and going was too ingrained in him. He had heard from Riordan earlier. Their mother was still alive but had been badly beaten. Riordan had hired a security company to provide protection for her and had lodged a complaint with the local police, not letting them get away with shoving it aside this time. He had threatened to go to the next level of law enforcement and saw the look on the police chief's face. He reported to Ciaran that the chief had quickly complied with his request.

MaKenna searched the kitchen, even as she opened the door to the outside for Emma.

Where was Ciaran? She looked at the clock, and sighed. It was so early. She wondered how her mother was and desperately wanted to talk to her brother. She wrapped her arms around herself as she paced, turning at one point to find Ciaran standing in the kitchen doorway, his hair still damp from his shower, his eyes on her.

He smiled and moved towards the counter, pointing at the chairs around the table. "Sit. Has Emma eaten? Then, sit. I have tea here for you."

She reached for the cup, her head tilting to study the china mug he had handed her, her hands wrapping around the warmth coming from it. "A China mug, Ciaran?"

He grinned as he turned from the toaster. "I keep it here for Mom. She likes her China mugs to drink from. She always has." When she went to speak, he held up a finger, shaking it at her. "We eat first. Then we talk. And yes, I have spoken with Riordan. Your Mom's is good hands."

Finally, MaKenna looked up at Ciaran, finding his eyes on her, a thoughtful look on his face.

"Can I call Riordan?" Her voice was hesitant, and it broke his heart to hear her pleading.

"We need to talk first, MaKenna. Come on. Let's go to the living room. Okay, we'll do the dishes first, then talk." He reached to stop her, pulling her into a hug. She was startled, then wrapped her arms around him, feeling safe for the first time in years.

Dishes in the dishwasher, all evidence of breakfast erased, Ciaran poured himself another cup of coffee. MaKenna had refilled her mug and was already sitting on the couch, her eyes on his laptop. He had left it there after working on it during the night.

He gave a quick prayer for guidance and wisdom, then sank onto the end of the couch, turning so he could face her. Now that he needed to talk to her, his words wouldn't come. He knew he had to talk to Art at some point that morning. He had received a text from him overnight, apologizing for setting in place what had happened.

"Ciaran? What aren't you telling me?" MaKenna was so afraid that her Mom was dead, even though he had said she was in good hands. And just where was her father right now? She needed to talk to her big brother, to hear his voice and his reassurances and yes, even his prayers. She had spent a long time the night before in prayer, finally surrendering everything she had gone through.

"MaKenna. I'm not sure where to begin." He paused, his eyes on the mug he was rotating in his hands before he saw her reach for it and put it on the table. "Okay. So, here's what I know so far. Your Mom's better this morning. The beating wasn't as bad as it looked. She does have a concussion, a couple of fractured ribs, cuts, bruises. No internal bleeding or injuries that they are worried about. Riordan says she'll be in the hospital for a couple of days. Then he's planning on having her moved to safety somewhere. He's not telling us where.

"Now about the police in your town. He threatened to go over their heads to the next level of law enforcement and ask for an investigation in the force. I think he still might. The police chief agreed to lodge a complaint of attempted murder against your Dad. Your Mom did tell your brother this wasn't the first time your Dad had hit her."

MaKenna's face showed her horror. "I knew it. All those times Mom made some excuse. I'm glad she's away from him. Go on."

He nodded. "Riordan said some other things, but I'll come back to that. I spoke with Art late last night. A patrol officer found your father's car in your driveway but didn't see him. Did he have a key to your house?"

She shook her head. "He wanted one but I made sure he couldn't get one at all. I kept my keys on me at all times. There is no way he had a chance to make a copy."

"They're looking for him. Now, about Anna. The text I got from Art said they had found her. She's okay, just very scared. She's been threatened and they're working on tracking back the threats to the source. Neither one of you will be in the office next week. He talked to the owners of the medical centre and let them know what you were both going through. You are both highly valued and they want you to stay safe. The locum coming in is aware of what is going on and has agreed that you two need to stay away from there for now. Mrs. Stirling is going in to work the office for him. She says she helped out before?"

MaKenna's attention was stopped at his question and she frowned. "I think she did, before I started. I know she did my training. Have they found Dr. Stirling yet?"

"They did, late last night. He was abducted from the office and put up a fight. He's hidden away for now." He paused, a thought coming to him. "How well did your Dad know him?"

Startled eyes flew to his and then she groaned. "That's how I got the job, isn't it? I thought I got it on my own merits, but he was still pulling the strings. I guess I'll be looking for another position when this is all over." She was growing angrier by the moment at her father and needed to let that go. She drew in some deep breaths and then sat back, visibly relaxing.

Ciaran watched her, compassion in his gaze. "Okay, then. You can always come work for me. I've seen the tools in your garage. Are you handy?" A cheeky grin peeked out and laughter danced in his eyes.

She smirked. "I am. Dad never knew that I would help a friend of Riordan's do renos when I was at college. That's how I managed to pay my way. When can I start?"

He waved his hands at her. "Hey! I was only kidding."

"I know, but I'm serious. I need to find work where Dad can't interfere. And sometimes tells me he can't with you."

Ciaran shook his head. "Okay, back to what we were talking about. I've been working on the papers and photos. I emailed some of the photos to Dad, and he's working through them as well. He said he's recognized a lot of the faces and is putting names to the faces for us, as well as their relationship. The thing of it is." Here he stopped, hesitating in what he needed to say. "He knows of your father. He didn't say how, but he'll email what he knows sometime today"

"Just what does your father do?" MaKenna had met his parents many times, but at that moment, realized she had never heard them say what his father did for a living.

"Did you never hear? He's a private investigator, working usually with financial institutions for financial fraud. He had training in forensic accounting and branched out on his own before Beth was born."

She nodded. "Then, get him to look into Dad's affairs, please. Somehow, this is just getting messier and messier."

He nodded, not telling her that his father had started that a couple of weeks ago and was finding out just how deep it went.

"Okay. Now about Uncle Timothy. Anything more on him?"

Ciaran shook his head, shooting a glance at the clock. Riordan would be calling in about thirty minutes and he still had to talk to MaKenna about something the two men had talked about.

Ciaran leaned forward to retrieve his coffee, taking a sip as he tried to organize his thoughts. What Riordan had asked seemed impossible, but it might be the only way to keep MaKenna safe and alive. He reached to stroke his hand down Emma's back and the dog leaned tight into him, her chin going to his knee, her eyes watchful and trusting.

"Ciaran?" MaKenna's voice held a question as she tilted her head to see his face. "You're troubled. Emma can tell. Why?"

He sat back, a sigh escaping from him. "Riordan and I had a very long talk during the night. He's worried about you, MaKenna. He's afraid your Dad will come and force you back home or to some location where he'll lock you up and throw away the key. He said he didn't realize how rough a life or how restricted a life you had when he left home for seminary."

She nodded. "Dad made sure he never knew. He threatened me, you know? He threatened to hurt Riordan if I ever told him what was going on." Tears sparkled in her eyes and she shuddered. "I couldn't let him do that."

"No, of course you couldn't. Riordan realizes that's what likely happened and it's breaking his heart." He paused, composing his lips together as he gathered his words. "Riordan has talked to Art, asking him to investigate your father in your uncle's death. He feels there's a connection somewhere. Something your Mom said last night triggered that. She has never known what happened to her brother, and they were very close, but something said last night makes her think your father was involved somehow."

She nodded. "More than likely he was. Anything we treasured or cared about was in danger from his anger. I can see him hurting or even killing Uncle Timothy." She glanced down at Emma, who sprang to the couch to curl up on MaKenna's lap. "He'll hurt Emma to get back at me. I know he will. He has hurt my pets in the past."

Sorrow wafted through Ciaran as she spoke. How could someone be so cruel? Lord, help me to control my anger towards him. I need a clear head. And my lady here needs a healing touch from You.

She was watching his face, he realized. He didn't cover what he was thinking very well, he knew, being too open with his thoughts and feelings. He reached for her hand, Emma reaching to nose both hands.

"Riordan is very much afraid of what your father will do if he catches you. First, do you have a boyfriend that you can turn to?"

She shook her head. "Dad made sure I never did."

"Good. I mean, not good that your Dad did that, but good that you're not in a relationship Now we need to make plans." He was still hesitant to bring up the plans Riordan wanted him to make. Knowing what she had gone through her whole life, he didn't want to push for something she might not want.

"Ciaran? What are you talking about? What plans does Riordan have?"

He sighed, his head dropping on the couch back as he slid his hands down his face. "He wants me to become your boyfriend. He thinks if I'm in your life, your father will back off."

"That won't work. He'll never back off for just a boyfriend."

"Fiancé, then?" When she shook her head, he spoke, his eyes not leaving hers. "What then? Husband?"

She stared at him, finally getting what he was asking her and what Riordan had been thinking. She froze, her thoughts wild. She nodded at long last. "I imagine that might be the only way, but there's no guarantee that would work. I can see him hurting or even killing a husband to gain control of me once more."

Ciaran nodded, not wanting to say what needed to be said. "Did you know you have a trust fund coming to you? The same with Riordan?"

She stared at him, shock on her face. "No. I never did. From who?"

"Your uncle. He left it in trust for you and your brother, payable once you reached a certain age. Twenty-seven for you is what your mother told Riordan. He says that happens in a couple of weeks, and once you reach that age, you both get your money."

She sat back once more, her hands resting on Emma. "I didn't know that. That's makes horrible sense, you know. Dad wouldn't like it that we had some money."

Ciaran blew out a breath, realizing she had no idea how much the trust fund was. "It's in millions, MaKenna. You won't have to work for the rest of your life."

She shot a startled look at him. "I'd give it all away to keep Dad from my life. But I guess that's not possible, is it?"

Ciaran shook his head. "We need to make some plans." He rose, reaching for their cups. "I'll be back with refills. Think about what you want to do."

He stood, hands resting on the counter as he waited for the new pot of coffee to finish. MaKenna's tea was finished, but he still hesitated to face her again. He heard soft footsteps, then a hand touching his back. He turned to he could face her, seeing the devastation in her face but also the resolve.

"So, what Riordan is suggesting is that I marry someone?" When he nodded, she paused, searching through her thoughts. "What happens to the trust fund if I die?"

"If you're not married, it goes to the other one of you. If both are dead, then it stays in trust forever, being paid out to charities. If you're married, it goes to your husband or to his wife in Riordan's case, if you have no children. If you have children, then it goes into trust for them. Your uncle was smart. He's set up trustees to manage it, people he trusted. If they're not able to, then there's a process in place to replace them. Your father can't get to it at all, unless he forces you to turn it over, and again your uncle put safety measures in place."

She sank into a chair at the table, giving a quiet thanks as he set her mug in front of her. Her thoughts were whirling. Ciaran stood, back to the counter, one hand gripping the edge, the other holding his own mug.

She finally looked up. "I gather you and my brother had a long talk last night." At his nod, she sighed, then continued. "I can guess what he asked you." She buried her head in her hands, overcome with everything Ciaran had said.

He set his mug down with a thump, angry at her father for causing this conversation in the first place. He crouched down beside her, reaching for her hands.

"Look at me, MaKenna." When she didn't, he reached a gentle hand to her chin and turned her face to him, his hand feeling rough on her smooth soft skin. "This is not something we do lightly. I've spent the night in prayer and know my answer. I ask that you do the same, spend time in prayer." His eyes searched her, trying to assess how she was feeling.

She sighed, even as she reached out a hand to touch his shoulder. "I know what and why this was asked. It would put you at great risk. And if we did this, it would tie us for life."

He nodded. "I realize that, MaKenna. Take some time to pray about it. I'll be in my office if you need me." He stood, reaching into his back pocket for his phone and setting it in front on her. "Riordan is calling in about fifteen minutes. Talk to him, too. We'll not rush into anything, love. Nothing at all. If we have to, we'll come up with another plan. This decision is yours, and yours alone. Don't let fear or panic push you. We'll deal with your father as we have to."

She nodded, her eyes on the phone, willing it to ring. She needed to talk to her brother and just hear what he had to say.

Ciaran watched her for a moment, then reaching to refill his mug, walked from the kitchen, heading for his office. He had work he needed to do to be ready for the next week, but he would be spending a good portion of time in prayer.

MaKenna watched him walk away, tall, strong, dependable, and wondered that God had brought him into her life at a time she needed him. She sighed, her eyes closing in prayer. He was right. She needed to pray. The phone chiming broke into her prayer.

✮ ✮ ✮ ✮ ✮

Ciaran looked up from the blueprints he was studying as he heard a sound at his office door and then sat back before rising to walk towards MaKenna. He dipped his head so he could see her face.

"MaKenna?"

"Ciaran! I don't know what to do! I talked to Riordan, but it just seems to extreme." Sobs broke out as she finished.

Ciaran reached for her, wrapping her in his arms, feeling that their time was running out and that danger was approaching far faster than either one of them realized. He had peeked out the front windows over the morning and studied the vehicle sitting in front of his house. Riordan had sent a text back to him, stating it likely was his father, watching to see if MaKenna was really there.

"Come, sit with me." Ciaran pulled her down on the couch beside him. "Now, talk to me." When she wouldn't, he spoke. "Then, I will. You've gotten counsel from your brother, who is also a pastor. You've been

123

praying. So have I." She went to speak and he laid a finger on her mouth. "Just let me speak for a moment." He paused to gather his words. "You've become a great friend to Beth. She has talked about you for months. I didn't meet you, just circumstances I would gather that prevented it. I feel like I know you. Having spent time with you in the last few days, I know that has changed. MaKenna, I love you."

She stared at him, her mouth slightly open, even as she shook her head. "It's too soon, isn't it?"

He shook his head in response. "If God has chosen us for each other, then time really doesn't matter, does it? What do you say? Will you honour me as my wife?"

The phone chiming interrupted them, and Ciaran dropped his head in frustration before reaching for it. His face whitened as he read it.

"This isn't good, MaKenna. Your father's figured out where you are. He's sitting outside right now."

"Ciaran! What are we to do?" She stood and began to pace. "How do I ever get free of him?"

He stopped her by stepping into her path. "Marry me, MaKenna. Let me deal with him."

She stared at him, before nodding slowly. "Okay. Then, my answer is yes." She studied his face, seeing the relief that flickered across it. "Now what?"

He spun, reaching for a desk drawer and drawing out a small box. "This was my grandmother's. Mom gave it to me. Will it do?"

He held up the blue sapphire ring, watching her face intently, breathing a sigh of relief as she nodded.

"It's beautiful, Ciaran. And in response to what you said, I do love you too. It just seems too quick."

He nodded as he reached for her, folding her into his arms and then pressing a kiss to her forehead. "We need to plan and plan quickly, I think. Riordan said he could get a marriage license for us. He has a friend here in town who would do that. Then, we could either have our minister do the wedding or he would."

"Our minister here, I think, Ciaran. I need Riordan here to support me." Tears sparkled in her eyes. "This is not how I thought I'd be planning my wedding, you know."

"I know, sweetheart. Listen, Mom and Dad are going to be home later today. Let me take you to Mom and she'll work with you. We need to do this soon. I just wish your Mom could be here."

Ciaran groaned as his phone rang and he reached for it.

"Art? I thought you had the day off."

Art's voice sounded rushed. "I was supposed to but something's come up. Where's MaKenna?"

"She's with me. Why?"

"Her home was broken into. We think it was likely her father. There doesn't seem to be any damage, but you can see where he's walked through the house. He didn't bother to clean the mud off his shoes."

Ciaran's eyes were on MaKenna as he spoke. "That doesn't surprise me. He's parked out front of my place now. Or he was." He walked through to peek out the front window. "No, his car's gone. He's in town somewhere."

"I know he is. And I spoke with her brother. He's heading this way with her mother and a security team. Is she safe?"

"She is, Art. I'll make sure she stays that way."

"Listen, if he's been parked out front of your place, then you two need to get out of there. Find some place safe for the day. I'll call back in a couple of hours." His voice cut off as he hung up.

MaKenna stood in front of Ciaran, waiting for him to speak. "What did he say, Ciaran?"

"Your father broke into your home last night. Nothing seems to be destroyed or missing. Art thinks we need to move from here."

She shuddered. "It's not going to end, you know. So now what?"

"Now, we gather up the papers that we're working on, find Emma's leash, and we go talk to our minister. Then I take you to see my parents."

"Your parents! What on earth are they going to say, Ciaran? We're practically strangers."

Ciaran broke up into laughter. "Not really. Beth has talked about both of us to the other. Besides, Mom and Dad can't comment. They only had a three week engagement, going together for only about three months before they married."

She looked shocked, then frowned. "Is this how it is with your family, you rush the brides?"

Ciaran laughed even harder as he reached for his sweetheart, enveloping her in his arms and kissing her for the first time. "No, we just know what we want and go for it."

"Thanks for the warning. It's a little late, you know." That earned her another kiss before he sent her to get ready to leave. He hesitated, staring at the papers he had been working on before gathering them quickly and stuffing them into the backpack. He called for Emma, fitting on her harness and leash, before heading for the door to the garage.

He turned as he heard MaKenna behind him and stopped, just taking in her beauty, before he reached for her hand and helped her into his truck. He looked around as he drove away, watching for the car he had seen, but not seeing it. He prayed that they would stay safe, that whatever it was they were facing would disappear but he knew it wasn't possible.

The man followed them, taking care that he didn't get too close. He knew her father was in town, and that complicated things. He would need to leave and let him run things and find the material he was sure the young couple had. If her father didn't leave voluntarily, then perhaps he wouldn't leave at all.

Ciaran's mother turned from her work in the greenhouse as she heard footsteps coming her way. Her face broke into a smile as she saw her son heading her way. She reached to hug him and then turned to MaKenna.

"Such a surprise to see you two here. Give me a moment and I'll be right in. Your Dad's in the house somewhere, Ciaran."

"Thanks, Mom." He turned to MaKenna. "Coming?"

She shook her head. "I'll come in with your Mom. I just want to walk through her greenhouse for a moment."

Anna turned to watch her, a puzzled frown on her face. Something was up with these two, more than what they had been told. She shrugged. Ciaran would tell her when he was ready. Then, she stopped as she watched MaKenna reach for a flower, her eyes on her hand. Then, she turned to face the house, her thoughts racing. That was her mother's old engagement ring on MaKenna's finger. What was going on with those two?

"MaKenna, I'm done in here now. Ready to head for the house?" Anna's smile was wide as she studied the younger woman walking towards her, almost in a hesitant manner.

"I am, Anna. Thank you for letting me wander around in here. This is something I've always wanted and never could have." A sadness tinged her words. She sighed as she thought back over her life and all that she had missed.

Anna drew MaKenna into a hug and, with an arm around her, led her back to the house. Ciaran and his father, Angus, were seated in the kitchen, cups of coffee in front of them and the open cookie tin between them. They had been in a heavy discussion by the sounds of it as the two women entered.

Anna and MaKenna moved quietly around the kitchen, preparing sandwiches and then seating themselves with the men.

Angus looked at his wife and then nodded at the younger couple.

"You two are up to something, I can tell. Spill."

MaKenna stared at him in shock as Ciaran and Anna laughed. Angus winked at her as he smiled.

"There is, Dad." Ciaran hesitated, his turning to the lady sitting beside him, even as he reached for her hand. "I asked, MaKenna said yes, and we have to plan a wedding."

His parents stared at the both for a moment before rising and hugging them both. Once seated, the parents shared a long look.

"MaKenna, this is sudden. You're sure?" Angus' voice was so much like his son's, MaKenna hesitated.

She shared a look with Ciaran even as she answered. "I'm sure. I know we haven't know each other long, but I understand that runs in the family." Anna and Angus laughed at that. "I know we love each other, we feel we have God's blessing, but there's more."

"Your father?" Angus' quiet voice broke through the emotions of the moment.

"Yes, that's correct, Dad. Riordan's found some more information that implicates him in the death of their uncle. From what I now understand, her father won't rest until he has her back home or worse. We feel that if we're married, he'll back off."

"Not necessarily, son. If it's to the stage I think it is, then he won't rest. Having you to protect her will help. But when and who?"

Ciaran groaned as his phone chimed and he pulled it out. "Riordan and your mother are heading this way. She's been released and the security team thinks she'll be safe here in our town." He glanced at her, seeing the steadiness of her gaze, before he continued, his eyes not leaving her face. "Her father was very restrictive. I won't go into the details now but MaKenna had no life. There's also a trust fund payable to both MaKenna and Riordan in two weeks or thereabouts. We're sure their father is after that, even though he can't get his hands on it."

"Well, that puts a different slant on it. If your mother and brother are to be here, then let's plan a wedding." Anna moved their plates to the sink and returned with a pad of paper and pen. "Go ahead. What are your ideas?"

They both laughed. "We haven't made any yet." MaKenna admitted. "We're heading over to talk to the pastor today if he's home."

"Actually, he's heading this way this afternoon, so that takes care of that. When were you thinking?"

"Tomorrow?" Ciaran shifted his chair as MaKenna jabbed him with her elbow. "Seriously, we're planning in the next little while. From what Art has said, it's crucial that we keep her as safe as we can. With our small town, people will talk if we spend our nights sheltered in the same house if we're not married."

"That's only part of it and you know that, Ciaran." His father stared at him until he nodded. "Now, let's get to work. How many are you planning for, where is the wedding, and where will you live?"

"Some of those questions we're working through. We both own homes, so either is an option." Ciaran stopped as MaKenna laid a hand on him.

"Your place, I think, Ciaran. I can't stay in mine anymore." She stared at him, a twinkle appearing in her eyes. "There's a huge problem though, that I don't think you thought of."

"And that would be? We've already considered how much in danger you are and what we need to do about that. We discovered we love each other and want to spend our days together. So, what's the problem?"

"Emma." Emma stood up with her paws on MaKenna's knee, between the two of them. "I hear tell you don't like dogs." She smirked as she said that.

"Emma? Dogs?" He stared down at Emma, who turned her head to him and then swiped her tongue across his face. "I like Emma. She's part of the package deal, isn't she?"

MaKenna's eyes softened as she smiled at him. The parents shared a look, remembering how they had had to compromise on things in the beginning.

"Okay. That's settled. Emma's part of the deal." Anna tapped the pad of paper. "Wedding dress?"

"I don't know. I like simple things. Dad threw Mom's dress out after they were married." Her face saddened. "Who knows what she's had to live with all these years?"

Anna's hand reached for her face and turned her to face her. "That's your mother's life. This is yours. Listen, I still have mine. I was about your size when Angus and I married. When we had our 25th anniversary, I could still fit into it. It's yours to use, if you wish. We'll take a look at it later." She speared her son with a look. "Now, Ciaran, how about you and Dad disappear for a while? Go find that detective and talk to him. Beth is heading this way this afternoon. Paul said he'd be here around 3. Did Riordan saw where they would be staying?"

Ciaran shook his head. "He wasn't sure."

"Tell them to come here, son. We've that bedroom here on the first floor. Their mother can use it."

He nodded and reached for his phone just as it chimed. He frowned, then excused himself to take the call.

"Come on then, MaKenna. Let's head upstairs to the guest room. You'll be staying here until your wedding. Beth is showing no signs of getting engaged so I'll be glad to let you borrow my dress." She stopped, turning on the wooden stairs to face MaKenna. "Just know that I don't want to step on your mother's toes and take over."

"Right now, Anna, you won't be. She's so beaten down, she's not thinking of anything but surviving. I don't know how I missed the signs all these years."

"Because it was you too. You made the step of making your own decision and leaving. That took a lot of courage." She paused, her eyes going to a picture hanging beside them, a picture of a tall, round tower. She pointed at it. "See this tower? I read about the towers in the Bible all the time. When I found this picture and wouldn't buy it years ago because I didn't think we could afford it, Angus bought it for me. He told me that the money for it didn't matter. What mattered what that I could look at it and remember that God is our strong tower. He protects us from all harm, walking through life with us."

MaKenna stared at the picture. "That's so sweet and that's exactly what we need to do."

MaKenna held her breath at the simple beauty of the gown, now ivoried, that Anna pulled out, slipping it over head.

"A near perfect fit, my dear. We can do alterations but I don't think we'll need to. If you were a bit of a higher heel, you'll be just fine. Now, no tears. We'll let your mom see you and see what she thinks."

MaKenna nodded, suddenly saddened at the turn of events. She knew she couldn't change them, but to hear her father wanted to harm her and would stop at nothing to do that hurt. Fathers weren't supposed to be like that.

"MaKenna, can I see you for a moment?" Ciaran stood at the bedroom door, his eyes on her, before he glanced at his mother, whose eyes narrowed at the look on her son's face. She sighed and then turned her thoughts to prayer. These two needed that right now, she thought.

"What's wrong Ciaran?"

"I just spoke with Art. He's on his way here. He has some new evidence he wants to present to us." He hugged her, his arms holding her tight. "I'm sorry, sweetheart. This should be the happiest time of your life and it's not. Maybe we should wait."

She shoved back from him, her hands on his chest as she glared at him. "Backing out, are you? That's not happening, boy."

He stared at her, his mouth open, until he heard his parents laughing and his father's comment about how she had told him.

"Then, I guess you still want to go through with this?"

"I do. No matter what happens, Ciaran, I want whatever time with you that God grants us."

He frowned at her words, then nodded. "Good. I spoke with Paul. He has what he needs to get a license for us and he is looking after that. He talked to your brother who hadn't had a chance to even look into that. He's almost here with your mom."

She nodded. "Then, I guess it's a trip downtown for us then. Thank you, Anna. We'll take up our plans when we come back."

"Just a minute, you two. You're rushing away from us. I just want to say something." They turned to look at Anna, questions on their faces. "If a meal doesn't matter, then let MaKenna's mom and I plan a simple meal. A cake is no problem. Mrs. B next door will do that today if I ask. Beth and Riordan will be here. There are flowers galore outside. What you two need to do is simply find rings for each other."

Angus stood behind Ciaran, reaching past him to draw the women forward, then praying for them all, his words resonating to the heavens. Ciaran brushed tears from his eyes, knowing that the support of his parents at this time meant so much. Please, Lord, let us solve this without hurt to MaKenna.

Chapter 10

$\mathcal{A}$rt Bourne stood waiting for them as they entered the police station, opening the door to the work area and leading them to a conference room, not his office. They stopped, staring at the activity going on there, and then at the pictures and notes taped up around the wall, their eyes stopping on the whiteboard, before turning to him.

"We've been busy, you two. I wanted you to meet the team working on this, so you can get a better understanding of how hard we're working for you. These people are involved in other cases as well, but are giving time to this as well." Art gestured around the room.

"How close are we to resolving this?" Ciaran wasn't sure if that was an appropriate question but he asked anyway.

"We're still in the process of collecting information, conducting interviews, waiting on forensics. At some point, day or night, someone is working this." He then led them back to his office, sighing as he sat. The work load just kept growing, even for a small town. He was tired and it was showing.

"You wanted to talk to us?" Ciaran watched the man, not quite sure what was up with him.

"I did. MaKenna, we know your father's in town. He has been spotted different times, but manages to elude whichever officer has seen him. We think he has help from someone in town, but we're not sure who."

She nodded. "And my mother and brother will be in town this afternoon. They'll be staying with Ciaran's folks." She held up a hand as he protested. "They have a security company with them on the way here. I'm not sure how long they'll be around."

Art nodded, knowing that he couldn't control that. "Now, about your uncle. We've talked to some people here who knew him. I hear he's left you and your brother trust funds." At her nod, he continued. "Is that what your father's after?"

She shook her head. "No, I don't think so but it's a possibility. What's set him off is that he can't control me any more." She shared a look with Ciaran. "And that's only going to get worse."

"Get worse?" He frowned at them, then groaned. "You two didn't, did you?"

"We are planning on getting married in the next few days, Art. You're welcome to come." Ciaran stared him down. "It's a step we've prayed about and are determined to take."

He nodded, knowing he couldn't change their minds. "That puts a different slant on it." He stared between the two of them. "Any other surprises?"

Ciaran shook her head. "We told you about the key. We're still trying to figure that out. I want to go back over MaKenna's house and see if there's something we've missed. Other than that, unless you've come up with a friend who has a lock that fits the key, we're at a loss. Dad's working on putting names to faces in the photos. He's also talking to a friend on the police force in MaKenna's town. The chief has been suspected in many things. Dad is gathering evidence and then will go to the law enforcement group that's higher than the force in that town and ask for an investigation."

"Good. If he needs help, let us know. We'll gladly lend our support." He looked around. "Now, if that's all, you two can head out. Just stay safe. I have no idea who all is after you two."

They stood for a moment outside the building before heading off downtown, hand in hand. Art stood for a moment, watching, then shaking his head, returned to his office. None of them saw the man standing watching, his eyes lifting to someone across the street, before he turned and followed them.

✯ ✯ ✯ ✯ ✯

Riordan stood in the hallway at Ciaran's parents' home that afternoon, looking lost and battered. The two mothers were in the bedroom set aside for his mother, the two younger ladies were upstairs. He could hear quiet conversation and laughter, no, giggles, he thought, wafting down the stairs. They were safe, so why did he feel to upset? He turned as he felt a hand on his shoulder. Ciaran's father stood there, pointing towards his office. Ciaran stood at the office entrance, watching as well.

"Come, son. Let's go sit and go over everything." Once in the office, he pointed at a chair, studying Riordan, noting the pain and stress marking his face, the fatigue weighing his movements. "Have you heard from your Dad?"

Riordan shook his head. "No. Not that I expected to. I only hear from him when he wants something." He pulled out his phone and checked it, frowning as he did so. "This is strange. A text message from a police officer I know at home." His hand froze as he scrolled through it, looking up at the two with me. "He says the police chief abruptly resigned, and he thinks is heading this way." His head dropped and he groaned.

Ciaran reached for his phone, looking at the text, then forwarding it to Art. "I've sent it on to Art. He'll make sure he's stopped before he does anything. Now, can you tell us anything different than what you did?"

Riordan shook his head. "No, I can't. I need to head out soon too. I have to be at the services tomorrow." He looked up, his eyes shuttered. "When are you planning the wedding, Ciaran?"

"We'll know better once Paul has arrived. He should be here soon. Can you wait?"

Riordan shook his head as he stood. "No, I should go now. I still have my sermon to finish for tomorrow." He barked out a laugh. "Who am I kidding? I haven't even started one."

"Then, just get up there and let God work through you. Use it as an opportunity to bring your people together, by sharing hurts, needs, encouragement, prayer." Angus stood and drew Riordan into a hug just as he would his own son. "We'll be praying for you. Come back as soon as you can."

Riordan nodded, dashing a hand across his eyes as he turned away, heading to find his mother and then his sister. Ciaran watched him walk away and then turned to his father.

"What do you think, dad?"

Angus shrugged. "It could be anything, this resignation, but I doubt it. I've been doing some research. He's dirty and has been for years."

Ciaran sighed. "Just what we need, another player in the mix." He shot a look at the door and then spoke. "We're planning on heading over to MaKenna's place to search again tomorrow. Want to join us?"

Angus stared at him for a moment, then nodded. "What's she doing about work? She can't go back to where she was."

"No, she can't. She's planning on helping me, if you can believe it."

Angus broke out into laughter. "Yep, that I can see. Come on. I'll be back in here working again tonight, and you can help. Right now, let's go find our sweethearts, get all gussied up and take them out for a meal. After we talk to Paul that is. I'm sure that's him now."

☆ ☆ ☆ ☆ ☆

Monday morning, MaKenna stared around the house Ciaran was renovating, moving to the side out of the way of the trades moving in and out. She didn't realize so much went on behind the scenes at a renovation. She felt out of place and realized she really shouldn't be here. She'd stick out the day and then find something else.

Ciaran watched her face from where he was talking to the plumber, knowing what was going through her mind. The two men reached an agreement and the plumber walked away, leaving Ciaran to approach MaKenna.

"Feeling out of place?" At her nod, he spoke. "It's not usually this bad. There aren't usually this many trades working at once, but we're on a time crunch here." He pulled her to the kitchen. "Here's something you can do. I need the pulls and knobs put on in here. If you can do that for me, I can go

146

back to work on the trim and hopefully finish it off today.”

“Are you sure I won’t be in the way?”

He shook his head. “Not at all. I’ll be more at peace and work better knowing you’re here.” He leaned back to look around and then leaned forward and snuck a kiss. “Besides, I can’t do this if you’re not here.”

She gaped at him for a moment, then laughed. “Go on, get to work.”

“Yes, ma’am.”

Later that day, they walked hand in hand into her home. Angus was to meet them there. Ciaran turned the key and then looked down at her.

“Are you sure about this, love?”

She nodded. “Let’s go through it thoroughly. Then the next time I come back it will be to pack it all up.” She drew a deep breath, shoved open the door and stepped in, her eyes searching room by room. She frowned. Something felt off, but she couldn’t be sure just what.

“Ciaran. I don’t like this. Something’s wrong here.”

“Wrong? What do you mean?” He stared at her, then began walking through the house. "I don't see anything, but if you think there is, then there is. Where do you want to start?"

She shrugged. "I have no idea." She spun in a circle, then frowned as she moved towards the panelling near her office. "This is a thick wall as well. I never realized it before." She paled. "There's not another body, is there?"

He wrapped her in a hug. "I pray not. Let's search. You take one side of the wall. I'll take the other. Dad should be here shortly. He used to come visit the couple that lived here, so he may have a better idea of where something could be hidden."

Ten minutes later, Ciaran heard MaKenna call his name.

"What did you find, MaKenna?"

"This part of the wood, whatever you call it, feels different from the other."

"The baseboard? Let me see." He pried at it. "You're right. Hold on a sec until I get my pry bar."

In short order, Ciaran had the baseboard loose and off the wall, reaching into the crevice. "I can feel something, MaKenna, but my hand's too big."

"Let me try." She reached in and pulled out a soft cloth bag. Loosening the top of it, she dumped out the contents. "Another key? Where does this one lead to."

Ciaran looked up as he heard noise at the front door. "Hide it, just in case." He quickly tapped the baseboard back into place and stood, reaching for her hand.

The man that appeared was the man who had accosted them before. "All right, you two. Enough is enough. Where's what was in that box?"

They looked at each other. "What would have been in that box?"

"Don't play innocent with me. I was watching and saw you remove something. Hand it over."

Ciaran backed up, putting MaKenna behind him. "There wasn't anything you'd be interested."

MaKenna screamed as the man's hand rose and fell quickly, the bat he was holding finding its place against Ciaran's head. Ciaran crumpled to the ground without a sound. MaKenna stood, frozen in place, her hands over her mouth, shock on her face as she stared down at him. She felt the man hard grip on her wrist pulling her towards him.

"You're coming with me until he turns over whatever it was you found." He stopped talking as he felt something poke himself in the back.

"I don't think so. Let the lady go." When the man's hand tightened, the voice spoke again. "Let her go. Now, hands on your head. I said, on your head." There was a sharp click of handcuffs and the man was being turned over to a patrol officer. Art turned from that to study both MaKenna and Ciaran.

Angus took a quick look at MaKenna. "Are you okay? Did he hurt you?"

She shook her head, rubbing her wrist as she did so. "Just the wrist. But he hurt Ciaran."

"I know. Art, can you watch for the paramedics, please?" Angus dropped down on his knees, his hands searching for the lump on his son's head and breathing easier as he found it not as bad as he expected.

"Is he okay, Angus?" MaKenna had crept to his side, worried about her man.

Angus wrapped an arm around her. "He is, MaKenna. He's unconscious, but I don't think it's that bad. Here are the paramedics. Let's move back. Art wants to talk to you."

She turned as Art approached, a frown on her face.

"How'd you come to be here?"

"Angus asked me to come. He had word that your father was near here."

"It wasn't Dad that did that. At least I don't think he was involved."

"You found something, didn't you, MaKenna?" Angus watched the conflict working its way across her face.

She sighed and reached into her pocket. "We found this in that bag over there, behind the baseboard. I had just dumped it out when he showed up."

"Is the first one you've found?" Art watched her face closely.

"No, it's the second key. The first one we found in a rusty metal box when Ciaran came to help clean up my yard after that windstorm. He got knocked down that time too by him."

"And you didn't think it was important to tell me that?" Art had trouble controlling his anger.

Her eyes shot to his and then they narrowed. "Frankly, we didn't think we had to. It was on my property, we didn't know who it was to press charges, and as far as we knew it had nothing to do with what's going on." Her own anger was rising, coupled with her fear about Ciaran. "I don't like your attitude. I'm not the suspect, in case you've forgotten. I put up with what you're dishing out from my father for years. I won't put up with it from you." She stormed from the room, following the stretcher carrying Ciaran and watched as it drew away. She returned to the room, quietly standing and watching the two men there.

Angus drew a hand across his face to hide his smile, admiration for her spunk uppermost in his mind. He winked at her, drawing a small smile from her Then, he turned to Art.

"She's right, you know. That may have nothing to do with what's happening. Or it could. May I see the key for a moment?"

Art nodded, his eyes searching the room they were standing in. What else would they find?

"I'd like to hold on to this. It's not evidence, not that you can keep at any rate."

"No, it's not. She's got a temper, doesn't she?" Art threw a glance back at the door and noticed MaKenna standing there for the first time. He winced as he thought of his words.

"She does. She's had a hard life that no one, other than her mother, ever knew about. From what she's told us, she was a virtual prisoner during her teen years." A commotion at the door drew their attention.

The two patrol officers outside were struggling with an older man, finally taking him down to the ground and handcuffing him. As they pulled him to his feet, spittle flying as he spat out his words.

"That's my father, Angus." MaKenna drew back to where she couldn't be seen.

"It's okay, MaKenna. You're safe. They'll take him downtown and book him for trespass and threatening to start with. Then, he'll be returned to your hometown to face the charges regarding your mother. You're safe from him." Art watched as she struggled to take it in.

"You're sure?" The hopeful look on her face broke Angus' heart and he reached to wrap an arm around her.

"I'm sure. It's this other thing you're involved in that I can't get a handle on."

"Somehow, I think it's all related to Dad. I don't think he ever liked Uncle Timothy. I was young, but I vaguely remember his telling Mom that her brother couldn't come around her. She used to sneak out to meet him. I can remember a couple of times doing that with her."

The two men with her shared a look. "We'll be talking to your mom, MaKenna. Maybe she'll have some more information as to what happened and how it's affecting you today." Art looked around. "Now what where you two doing here today?"

She sighed, wanting to be at the hospital, not here answering questions. "We were looking for a lock. But please, can we talk later. Here's my keys. Lock up and get them back to me. Angus, can we leave now?"

He nodded, just waiting to have a quick word with Art, before tucking MaKenna into his car and heading for the hospital, worry now coming to the forefront.

An hour later, MaKenna stood, her hand in Ciaran's as he opened his pain-filled eyes and looked around, groaning as he realized he was in the hospital.

"What happened?"

"Art and your Dad arrived in time to arrest the man. They also arrested Dad when he showed up."

"Is it over?"

She gave a low laugh at his hopeful words. "No, not yet. We still haven't solved the mystery of the keys."

"Good, I'm glad. Tell me what we found when I wake up." He drifted off to sleep, leaving MaKenna staring at him, openmouthed.

Angus gave a bark of laughter. "He'll not remember what he said, but you remember and use it against him one day."

She shook her head at him. "Did he really just say that?"

He nodded. "Look, I know you want to stay. Riordan's on his way. I'll leave once he's here."

Chapter 11

*R*iordan stood, watching his sister as she moved around her home, trying to pack but not getting very far. Something was up with her, but he wasn't sure what. He realized he hadn't know her as well as he thought all those years, she had hidden the secret of what she went through too well. Lord, help us to reach her. Show her that strong tower she can run to.

"MaKenna? Are you packing or just shifting stuff around?"

She sighed as she turned to him. "I think I'm just disturbing the dust, that's what I'm doing. This is hard, you know, Riordan."

"I know it is. You've planned a wedding for this week in only a week, you're not sure if you're doing the right thing, and we have the trouble with Dad hanging over our heads." He approached her and hugged her. "Now, what can I do?"

"Look for a keyhole."

"What?" He stepped back, eyebrows raised as her comment.

"I'm serious. That's what Ciaran and I were doing yesterday when he got hurt. I know he went to work today and shouldn't have. His mom went over to make sure he took it easy tonight. Beth is with our Mom, and his Dad is deep in research out of town. That leaves just you and I."

"And how do you think we'll find a keyhole?"

"By looking, Riordan. How else?"

He nodded, then looked around. "Where did you two start?"

"Along the hall way of the office. I don't think Ciaran had gotten too far when I found the baseboard that I did." She frowned, spun around and headed back for the office. "There's something about this room that's bugged me since I moved in, and I'm not sure why."

"Okay. Close your eyes." She stared at him for a moment. "Remember what we used to play with Mom when we were kids? She's show us something real quick, and we'd have to describe it to her. We always found closing our eyes was best."

"You're right. I had forgotten." She handed him a pad of paper and pen. "You can be my scribe. Write down what I say."

He nodded, and stood, pen posed over the paper. She closed her eyes and thought, beginning to describe the empty room she first saw. Her voice hesitated for a moment, and her eyes opened as she turned to face the wall that sat between the office and the kitchen. "That wall, Riordan. Something about that wall. That's what's off."

He nodded and set down the pen and paper, heading that way. "There's a lot of decoration on this wall that isn't in any other room. Now, I wonder why." He touched a piece of moulding and it turned, revealing a key hole. He spun, his eyes bright with interest. "Do you have the keys?"

She nodded as she dug them out of her pocket. "Here."

He tried them but neither moved the lock. He studied the lock and then the keys. "These aren't the right keys. There has to be another one somewhere."

"And I have no idea where." MaKenna moved to feel along the other mouldings. "None of these seem to move." She turned and walked to the doorway. "Now I wonder."

Riordan watched as she walked from the room, then hurried after her. He watched as she stopped in front of the mantle. "I wonder, Riordan, if there's something here."

"It seems that it would be too obvious, don't you think?"

She shrugged. "Why not put something in an obvious spot? Would you have searched here?"

He shook his head. "Not likely. But you would."

She grinned back at him even as a piece of wood moved. She reached for the keys, plucking them from his hands. The first one turned the lock, and she caught her breath.

"Let me, MaKenna. Do you have a flashlight?"

She nodded, running for her bedroom and back, handing him the light she kept by her bed.

Shining it into the cavity, he reached in and pulled out a small metal tin.

"That's like the one we found outside. What kind of game is going on here, Riordan?"

"I have no idea." He pried off the lid to find another key, this time with a note.

"It's a map of some kind, isn't it?"

He nodded. "It is. It's strange why they would hide it there."

"Ciaran found something similar the day we cleaned up the old shelving and he measured for the new ones. I'm not sure where he put it."

"It will be around somewhere. We can ask him tomorrow. Let's see if this key fits the other lock."

Disappointed that it didn't, the siblings cleaned up and headed back to Angus and Anna's, anxious to see how their mother was, not surprised to find Ciaran ensconced on the couch. He reached a hand for MaKenna and drew her down to him. She sat on the floor and they talked quietly, Riordan standing and watching for a moment before he walked away to find his mother.

MaKenna watched Ciaran's face as she described what they had found. A frown appeared, and he shifted to a sitting position, drawing her up to sit beside him.

"A map? Was it like the other one?"

She shrugged. "I can't remember exactly what that one was like." She reached into her jeans pocket to pull out the map that had been found that day. "Here. Maybe you remember."

"I don't really. But it's on Dad's desk." He made to rise, but stopped when MaKenna's hand rested on his arm.

"Sit. It's not important right now. We'll let your Dad look at them."

He turned to watch her, a frown on his face. "You're up to something, love. Care to share?"

She shook her head. "Just an idea I had. Do you know if the homeowner owned a boat or a cottage or cabin?"

He shrugged. "Dad might remember. I don't know that they did but this close to Lake Erie? He might have done so. Are you thinking that's where the keys belong?"

"It's just a thought."

Riordan hesitated in the doorway, watching his sister and her soon-to-be husband. He had so wanted to be a part of her life, to watch the love develop between these two and it had been denied him. He raised his eyes to the ceiling, even as his heart in its hurt cried out. He had no idea what they would be facing in the near future, but he knew it would be bad. He had talked to Art earlier and the news was not good. His father had somehow escaped from jail in their hometown. They figured he had help to do that, but everyone was denying being involved.

Ciaran looked up at that point, catching the look on Riordan's face and frowned.

"Riordan? You don't look very happy. What's up?" Ciaran's voice broke into his thoughts.

He sighed as he came into the room and sat, not sure how to proceed. "I just got off the phone with Art. He says he tried to reach you, Ciaran, but couldn't."

Ciaran searched for his phone. "I don't have my phone. Where did I leave it?"

"I think you left it at my place, perhaps?" MaKenna went to stand, intending on heading there.

"No, I had it here today. Just not sure where I left it." He groaned as he moved. "I think it's in Dad's office and likely muted."

Riordan nodded. "We'll get it later. Art had some bad news. Dad escaped."

"How could that happen?" MaKenna was on her feet, pacing. "I thought it was all over with him."

"Not likely, MaKenna. They're looking for him and hope to find him, but he's hiding and hiding with help."

"The police chief?" Ciaran made the suggestion, knowing full well it was likely true.

Riordan nodded. "That's what they think and somewhere here in town." He paused before he continued. "Somehow, I don't think you getting married is going to make any difference, MaKenna."

"Not likely, but he won't stop me. So now what? We continue to hide, to look over our shoulders, wait for the other shoe to drop, not get on with our lives?"

"All of the above for now, love." Ciaran stood, grimacing at the movement. "But first, let's go talk to Dad. He may have some ideas on what to do."

☆ ☆ ☆ ☆ ☆

Ciaran turned from where he stood in his parents's backyard that next Saturday morning, his father standing beside him and Paul the minister waiting. He drew in a breath as he saw Beth walking towards him and then his eyes caught sight of MaKenna on Riordan's arm as she walked towards him.

She is a beautiful lady, he thought, and she's mine.

The ceremony and dinner over, MaKenna and Ciaran stood hand in hand in his parents' driveway, waiting for goodbyes to be said. They had planned on just slipping away but that didn't happen. Ciaran was due to start another renovation on Monday and MaKenna would be right beside him, working as best she could. Emma was safe with Beth for the weekend.

Monday night, MaKenna turned to Ciaran as he studied the blueprints of the new renovation. She rubbed her hand along his back before stopping beside him.

"Do you think Dad is still out there somewhere?"

Ciaran raised his head. "I know he is. He has eyes all over this town now, I'm thinking. I don't know how we'll ever stay safe."

"Art is looking for him but he told me today that if something doesn't break soon in the case, they'll have to move on to another one. It's hard to hear that."

Ciaran nodded, his eyes on her face. "It is. We'll keep looking. Dad was still working on finding more property that couple owned."

She frowned. "I know he is, but something tells me any property would be well hidden. I think the key, pun intended, is back at my place."

"I'm sure it is. You haven't had any more parcels or text messages, have you?"

She stopped in her walk back to the kitchen and turned, a puzzled look on her face. "Now that you mention it, I haven't. But then, I wouldn't know, would I, as you still have my phone."

"I do, don't it?" Ciaran moved past her to his office, returning with her phone. "I've had it shut off since you gave it to me. We'll need to charge it likely before it boots up."

She froze. "I'm not sure I want to do this. I'm not sure I want to hear any messages he's left for me."

"You're not alone this time, love. How long will it take to get enough charge to turn on?"

"Give it thirty minutes." She walked away. "If there's anything there, pass it on to Art. I don't want to hear it or read it."

Ciaran watched her walk away, then turned his attention to her phone, willing the next thirty minutes to speed by. He pulled up her text messages, anger growing as he read them. He shot a look at the kitchen, and then pulled up her voice mail. He knew she had accessed it but had saved any she thought he should heard. His face paled as he heard the threats, not just from an unknown male but from her father as well. He pocketed the phone, intending to hand it over to Art the next day.

"Ciaran, can you come here for a moment?"

Ciaran headed for the backyard, greeting Emma as she headed towards him with her ball. She shot down the yard after it when he threw it, excited yips filling the air.

"What is it, love?" Ciaran's arms went around his wife as she stood staring at the back garden.

"Someone's been here. Look!"

Ciaran followed her finger and froze. Someone had been there and left a package for them. He pulled out his phone and called Art. They weren't safe here, either, as much as he wanted to believe that they were.

Art stood, holding the open package, staring first at them and then into the box.

"You didn't touch it? Okay, then he's been following you a lot closer than we thought. What we have here are pictures of your wedding and then you two at work today, going by the time stamp."

MaKenna shuddered. "Still? I had prayed it would be over when we got married. Obviously it's not. What does he want?"

"Whatever it is he thinks you have, he's not going to give up until he has it. Any ideas of what?"

MaKenna shook her head. "All we have are keys to locks we have no idea about."

Ciaran hugged her tighter and then pulled out her phone. "There are a number of text messages and voice mail messages you need to listen to. He's escalating in his threats towards us. I just wish I knew who it was."

Art took the phone, turning it over and over in his hands. "I have your permission, MaKenna to listen to and read the messages?" At her nod, he sighed. "I'll have you sign a waiver just for legality. I just wish it was over, and we had the culprit in handcuffs."

"Art, you grew up around here. Did you know the previous owners to my home?"

He nodded. "I knew of them. Used to serve him gas back when I was in high school and worked at the local gas station. Why?"

"Did they own any other property other than the house?" MaKenna and Ciaran shared a look.

Art frowned. "I think they did, a cabin or a cottage or something like that. Why?"

"We're wondering if the keys might belong to another property. We've found to maps, and one has a set of numbers on the back." MaKenna stopped her words at the look on his face.

"You've found two maps, and didn't bother to tell me?"

"I'm sorry. The first one I didn't even think about. We found it near the wall we tore down. It must have been tucked behind one of the shelves. The second one Riordan and I found in a compartment in the fireplace mantle. With everything that went on, I didn't think of it connecting to this."

Art nodded, his mouth tight. "From now on, you share anything you find with me. It could cost you your lives if you don't."

MaKenna nodded as she looked at Ciaran. "We will. It's just that I never thought of them being important to you."

"Anything small could be the trigger that solves this. I'll get back to you on properties. If I do, I don't want you two running off on your own to investigate. Do you hear me?"

"We won't go anywhere that you have jurisdiction over. We promise." Ciaran crossed his fingers behind his back, hoping that Art overlooked his wording. He drew a sigh of relief when he nodded and walked away.

"Ciaran? What did you mean?" MaKenna's voice was a low whisper.

"I meant what I said. He doesn't have police jurisdiction outside of the town limits. If we find something to look at out in the area around the town, we won't be stepping on his toes. Now that he's said something, I'm going to see if my friend can do a title search for me."

"And find the properties. What if they're occupied?"

"Then we leave it. If they're not, or only vacation rentals, we'll see what we can do."

Ciaran went looking for MaKenna the next day on the job site, not finding her. He searched outside. His truck was there, so she had to be somewhere there. He walked around the outside of the one-storey house and into the garage, holding onto the doorframe as he leaned in to look around. She wasn't there. Puzzled, he turned in a circle, then headed back into the house, even searching the basement. She had disappeared. He searched for a note and saw nothing. Then, in the sawdust on the front porch, he saw the footsteps. MaKenna's mixed with a larger size, that of a man's. It looked as if she had struggled. He sank to the floor, his heart in his mouth, prayers raising to heaven even as he pulled out his phone to make the call he had prayed he would never have to make.

Art stood near Ciaran, listening as he gave his statement to the responding officer, then turned and walked through the house, seeing where Ciaran had been working. He turned, with a frown, to study the front door. The man was bold, he'd give him that, to come up and abduct MaKenna when Ciaran was so near at hand.

"Art?"

He turned as he heard Ciaran's voice. "Ciaran. I'm sorry. I thought you two would be safe if you were together."

"I know. So did I. I didn't hear a thing. I had ear protection on while I was working. And I only had it on for about five to ten minutes, max."

"Just long enough for her to disappear. We'll find her, Ciaran. We have some planning to do now. Some equipment to set up at your place. Where's your phone?"

Ciaran reached for it and froze. "I gave it to MaKenna this morning. We haven't replaced hers yet and she wanted to talk to Riordan." His eyes slid closed as he realized they had no way to reach him. "Now what?"

"Now we get you another phone and text that number to yours. Chances are they have already found it." Art turned to speak to one of the officers, then pointed at the door. "You drive. I rode with the patrol officer."

Chapter 12

*T*wo weeks had passed by. Ciaran dragged himself to work and home again, filling in as long a day as he could. He was losing weight, not sleeping. His only comfort was Emma, who stuck close to him when he was home, curling up beside him wherever he sat, and laying as tight to him as she could get at night. She missed her mistress, that much was obvious.

His family had tried to help him, as had Riordan and his mother, Sarah. Nothing worked. He spoke daily with Art and the other detectives but they had no news. There had been sighting of her father and he wasn't sure if that was good or not. He knew her birthday was in a couple of days. He had had great plans for it, plans he now looked at with sorrow and wondered if he would ever get to put them into action.

He drew strength from his prayer and Bible study, finding that strong tower he so desperately needed to hide in. And that's what he felt he was doing, hiding.

He turned as he heard footsteps on the grass coming towards him. He had been sitting on the grass in the backyard, idly throwing the ball for Emma. His father stood for a moment before lowering himself to the ground and then just sat, without saying a word.

"How are you, son?"

Ciaran shrugged. "I don't know any more, Dad. Everyone asks that and I don't have an answer."

"I know you don't. Just say you're don't know how you are. Your friends will understand." His father stretched his legs out in front of him, leaning back on his hands, ducking his head as Emma moved in to sniff his face and then deliver a lick.

"I've been doing more research, son, and I think I've found one of the houses. It's an abandoned cabin about thirty minutes from here. Tomorrow's Saturday. How be we take those keys and see if one of them fits the lock?"

Ciaran drew a deep breath. "I'd be glad to do just that, Dad. I can't just sit here but I have no idea where to look for her. I keep sending text messages to my phone, hoping they reach her, but Art thinks they took the number of my new phone and then trashed my old one."

"That they may well have done. We'll take a look in the morning and see what we can find. I haven't spoken to Art, but I did call Riordan and ask him to pray for us tomorrow." He sighed, not knowing how to go on. "He wanted to come but can't."

"He has responsibilities that he needs to take care of. When and if we need him, then we'll bring him here. How's Sarah? I have talked to her today."

"She really hurting, blaming herself for not leaving him earlier. But I don't think it's her father, unless he's somehow mixed up in this."

"I don't get that feeling either." Ciaran stood. "What time in the morning, Dad?"

"Around eight, I think. Will Emma be okay on her own here?"

Ciaran nodded. "She should be. If we're too long, Beth will come and look after her."

The next morning found the two men driving quickly from their town, heading towards a small village thirty minutes from there. Angus stopped on the outskirts of the village to check his map, then paused.

"Ciaran, do you have the copies of those maps with you?"

Ciaran shook his head, bringing his mind back to where they were. "I do. Why?" He reached for his wallet, pulling out the folded papers.

His father took them, unfolded them, then tapped the first one they had found. "I thought this one looked familiar. It leads to the old Pierson place."

"The Pierson place? Isn't that where you used to take us to get apples in the fall?"

Angus nodded. "It is. Let's hope we find something there today. I have to be in the city next week to testify at that court hearing."

"I know. Mom's going to miss you, you know."

Angus grinned. "I know she will. But it's you we're concerned about. We need to find your wife."

Ciaran leaned forward as he father drove as far as he could down the overgrown lane, finally stopping when he could go no further.

"I don't see that anyone has been down here lately." Ciaran stood by the car and looked around.

"No, I don't they have been, but I think there's another laneway. I'm just not sure where it is. Come on, son. Let's see what we can find."

Ciaran stood staring at the dilapidated building, the siding weathered and gray, chunks breaking off from around the windows and doors. There was no door left and all the windows were broken. He raised his eyes to the roof and assessed it. It was in bad shape, he thought.

"Dad? Do we go in?"

His father shook his head. "I'm not sure that it's safe. Where are the keys?"

Ciaran held them up and his father reached for them. "These don't look like a normal house door key, more like a padlock one of sorts. Now where would they put a padlock?" He turned to study the area, finally heading for a nearby shed.

"This looks as if someone's been around here recently. The brush has been beaten down."

Ciaran held his breath as his father reached for the old rusty weathered padlock and inserted the first key, withdrawing it to insert the other. He struggled for a moment and then the lock snapped open. He pocketed the key even as he reached to pull the padlock free. He waited for a moment, watching Ciaran as he did so.

The door swung open with a loud squeak, the hinges old and rusty. They waved away the cobwebs hanging in front of them and then stepped in, their eyes searching in the dimness. Dust motes floated downwards in the streaks of sunlight pouring in through the cracks in the walls and roof.

Ciaran paced around, trying to figure out what the reason was for the key being hidden.

"Do you see anything, Dad?" He turned when his father didn't answer.

Angus held up a metal box. "This. We'll take it with us. It wasn't hidden well, but blended in with the dirt floor unless you were looking for it." He turned in a circle, taking in the debris and destruction wrought by the insects, animals and weather. "I don't see that MaKenna was here at all."

"No, I don't think she was. I was so hoping we'd find some evidence that she was." Ciaran's voice died away as he walked towards the back wall and then bent to pick up something. "Dad!"

Angus spun at the anguish in his son's voice and moved rapidly towards him, his hand coming down on Ciaran's shoulder. He searched his son's face, then stared at the object in Ciaran's hand.

"Is that a shoe?"

"It is, Dad. It's MaKenna. She was wearing them to work and accidentally stepped into some paint. She got it off the sole but left the top, saying it made a statement."

Angus sighed. "Then, we'll need to all the police after all."

"What about the box, Dad? Will we have to turn it in?"

Angus studied it. "Let's open it first, son, and see what's in it." He worked to open the rusted metal, praying they'd find something. It was empty and had been for a while by the looks of it. He felt inside to make sure he hadn't missed anything. "If there was anything here, it's long gone. I would say the box has been there for years."

"How do we explain us being here?"

"I had permission from the lawyer overseeing this property to be here. He knew what we were looking for. He's searching for more property for us."

"You didn't tell me that, Dad."

"I didn't because I didn't want to get your hopes up. Tell you what. When we get home, let's take that other map and see if we can match it to an area around here."

Ciaran nodded even as he heard the voices of the approaching officers. It would be a while before they got out of there, he knew, and they were no further ahead in finding MaKenna or even solving who was after them.

Days later, Angus knocked on Ciaran's door, suppressed excitement in his manner.

Ciaran stared at him, then stepped back to he could enter. Emma stood on her hind legs to greet him, then seeing it wasn't her mistress, walked away, her head down, her demeanour depressed.

"She's not happy, is she?" Angus' question seemed to come out of the blue.

"No, she's not. She's really missing MaKenna." His eyes slid shut to block the tears shimmering in them.

"It's okay to cry, son. We all do at some point or other."

"I've never seen you cry, Dad."

"I have, many times over the years, son. It's usually been when I'm on my own or after you kids had gone to bed."

"So the saying that real men don't cry isn't true?"

"Not at all. We just handle things differently. Never be afraid to cry, especially in front of MaKenna. It draws you closer together and closer to God. Remember that Jesus wept."

"That He did. I forget that, you know. Now, what brought you here?"

"I found the other property, but I have to wait for clearance from the lawyer. He found it buried in the paperwork. He just needs to verify that it's not occupied. I spoke with him late this afternoon."

"It's Friday tomorrow. Can we go Saturday?"

"If all goes well, we can. You've had no word yet."

"No. It's as if they know we haven't found anything yet."

"That they may do. I'm sure you're being watched and I would suspect we are as well." He turned as a knock came to the door. "Were you expecting anyone?"

Ciaran shook his head. "No, unless it's Art. And it is Art." He pulled the door open on the detective.

"And it is Art. New kind of greeting?"

Ciaran smiled as he shook his head. "No. Dad asked if I was expecting anyone and I said no unless it was you. Come on out to the kitchen. I have coffee on the go." As they were seated, Ciaran stared at Art. "What brings you out here tonight?"

"I can't just come and see how a friend is?"

"Not buying that. Spill why you're here."

Art laughed, then sobered. "We're still getting text and voice mail messages on MaKenna's phone. We're following up on them. It doesn't appear that whoever has her is the doing this."

"I think, if you track it back, it will be her father or someone he's hired. She was leaning that way and was getting ready to confront him."

"That's our feeling too. He's been spotted here in town and we're hopeful that we'll find him in the next couple of days."

Ciaran nodded, the words small comfort. "If it's not him, then we don't know who it is or why."

"Not quite true. Our investigators have some theories and are working through them. We can't discuss them just yet."

Angus watched his son's face. "Let them work on this, Ciaran. We have something else we're working on."

"That we do. Thanks for the reminder, Dad."

Art stood, his thoughts open on his face. "Whatever it is you two are up to, please stay safe and stay within the law."

Ciaran walked him to the door and then came back to sit down at the table. His heart was hurting and he couldn't hide the hurt. His father watched him, his heart hurting for his son, before he rose and refilled their cups with coffee. He sat back down, sitting in silence with his son. They needed to make plans for Saturday, but right now all he could see was his hurting son and this time, he couldn't make it better.

"So, Dad. Are you sure we can gain access to this property?"

"We can." He reached for his phone. "It's set. We have permission to go in on Saturday. I just pray this time we find something."

"Me, too, Dad. I can't take much more." He rose to let Emma back in, reaching to pick her up in his arms. She nestled down with her chin on his shoulder. His head went down as his tears wet her coat.

☆ ☆ ☆ ☆ ☆

Ciaran stood, that Saturday morning, in front of an old abandoned sawmill. He turned in a circle, searching, but not finding anything. His father worked at the door, finally pulling it open, the bottom of it digging into the dirt and debris packed against it. He followed his father in, reaching to brush away cobwebs, before stopping, staring at the skeletons of the machinery abandoned and rusty now from the elements and neglect.

"Are you sure this is the place, Dad?"

Angus nodded. "I'm sure, son. Come on. You take that side. I'll take this side. Shout out if you find anything."

"This will take more than one day, won't it?" Ciaran was discouraged.

"Take heart, son. Every time we rule out something, we're getting closer to her." He watched as Ciaran finally nodded his head and walked away, his head moving from side to side as he searched. Angus sighed, then turned to his own search, finding nothing until he came to a locked door. He reached for the key he hadn't returned to Ciaran the previous week and inserted it into the lock. With some jiggling and a little pressure, the lock clicked open.

With a prayer on his lips, he pushed open the door, staring in wonder at the room in front of him. He heard footsteps behind him and then Ciaran's voice.

"What is this room, Dad?" His father's hand stopped him from entering.

"I don't know, son, but we go no further. Look at that equipment there. I suspect it was for printing counterfeit bills. And I can see evidence that drugs were run through here." He turned and pointed to the door. "We leave now. Did you find any evidence that MaKenna was here?"

"None. I don't think she was." He stopped and turned back to stare at the open door. "There has to be something more there if that man was going to these lengths to get the keys for this room."

"I'm sure there is. Now, let's get out of here."

He pulled out his phone, contacting the lawyer to let him know what he had found and then calling in law enforcement. He sighed. This was not what he had been expecting to find. He had prayed that they would find MaKenna.

Chapter 13

MaKenna slumped down on the thin dirty ratty blanket she had been given. She just knew this was it. She strained to see if any daylight was coming in around the door but couldn't see any. There were no windows in the room she was in, just a toilet in the corner. Once a day, a man appeared with just enough food for one meal and two bottles of water that had to do her for the whole day. She was dirty, tired, discouraged.

Lord, she prayed, I have no idea where I am or why. But You do. Is this was dying is like? She curled up on the blanket. She had quickly learned that it was better to have it between her body and the floor. She wrapped her arms tight her and tried to sleep. That seemed to be the only escape she had. She had no idea how many days had gone by. A short harsh cough shook her body. Lord, please don't let Ciaran grieve for too long. Make sure he knows I love him dearly. Her eyes closed and she drifted off, certain that this was it for her.

She didn't hear the sirens approaching, didn't hear the heavy booted footsteps that searched the building, didn't hear the shaking of the door and padlock, didn't hear the shouts for a pry bar or the harsh rending of wood as the lock was pried off. She didn't see the bright sunlight that shot through the door as it was slammed back.

Art stood in the doorway for a moment, his eyes adjusting to the dimness of the room as he searched it, anger building inside him. His eyes swept the room and then dropped to the floor. A shout for the paramedics, and he was on his knees beside her, reaching for her neck to feel for a pulse. He sat back on his feet, thankfulness coursing through him that he had found her.

He rose and stepped back, watching as the paramedics worked to stabilize her before lifting her to a stretcher, oxygen mask in place, an IV line running to her arm. At his questioning look, the senior paramedic shook his head.

Art followed them to the ambulance, calling for one of the patrol officers to climb in.

"Call me as soon as you have word." He spun, knowing he would be tied up there for hours, but he needed to call Ciaran.

Pulling out his phone, he turned it over and over, not sure of the words he needed to find to let the young, newlywed husband know he had found his wife, but he didn't know if she'd survive her ordeal or not. He called Angus instead.

"Angus?"

"Art? You're putting in a lot of hours this week."

"I know. It's been one of those weeks." Art squinted against the sun as he watched the crime scene team approach. "Listen, is Ciaran with you?"

"He is. Why?"

"Can you put your phone on speaker, please?"

"Art?"

He could hear the question from Angus and the dread in his voice. "Just do it please." He heard the echo that comes when a speaker phone is activated.

"Art? Dad said you wanted to speak with us." Ciaran's voice was flat.

Art sighed inwardly. "I did, Ciaran. Where are you two?"

"We're at Dad's, trying to figure out the next step. We found another building that fit the other key and spent the day there. Why?"

Art swallowed against the lump in his throat. "I found her, Ciaran. I found MaKenna."

There was silence on the other end of the phone. He wasn't sure if they had heard him correctly. His mouth opened to speak again when he heard Ciaran speak.

"You found MaKenna? Is she okay?"

"I did, Ciaran. She's on her way to the hospital. It's not good. She's in rough shape." He paused, not wanting to go into the details yet.

He waited as he heard the sobs from the other end of the phone. *Dear Lord, I don't believe much, at least I never had. But this is a miracle You worked out. Help me to believe. Be with these friends of mine.*

"Art?" Angus' voice was thick and rough. "Which hospital?"

"Ours, for now. If they have to, they'll transport her. Go. Be with her."

Placing his phone on the table, Angus reached for his son, drawing him into his arms. Ciaran clung to his father in a way he hadn't since he was a small boy. Angus looked up as he heard footsteps. Anna and Sarah stood there, questioning looks on their faces, until he nodded. They turned to each other, both mothers in tears.

Finally, Ciaran sat back, swiping at his face. His father reached for a dish towel and handed it to him.

"Get yourself together a bit, son. Then we'll head for the hospital."

"She's alive, Angus?" The anguish in Sarah's voice cut through the sorrow in the room.

"She is, Sarah. Art found her. She's likely at the hospital now. Come on. Let's get over there to our girl." He reached for his phone. "Grab your stuff. Come on, son. Up on your feet. Let's go."

He paused long enough to call both Beth and Riordan and then Paul. He followed the women out to the car, his heart hurting. He had heard in Art's voice what he didn't want to verbalize.

Ciaran almost ran into the Emergency Department and slid to a halt at the clerk's desk. She looked up, a frown on her face.

"My wife?"

"Ciaran? Who's your wife? I didn't know you were married." Eva had gone to school with him and was jealous of any girl that he had talked to.

"MaKenna? They just brought her in."

"MaKenna? Oh yeah. Just have a seat. The doctor's just gone in with her."

"No, you don't get away with that, Eva. I want to see her and see her now."

"It doesn't work that way, Ciaran. Sit or I'll call security."

A voice spoke from behind Ciaran. "Open the door, Eva. That's enough."

She shot a glare at the security guard , a friend of Angus who knew what had been going on, standing behind Ciaran and complied.

With a quick word of thanks, Ciaran headed for the rooms at the back. Angus, Anna and Sarah stood and watched before finding seats.

"Ciaran?" The Emergency Room doctor looked askance at him. "What are you doing back here? I don't think we have any of your family here, do we?"

He nodded, hardly able to speak. "Makenna? They just brought her in. She's mine." He swallowed hard. "She's my wife."

"MaKenna." He spun to stare at a curtained room. "In there. But wait. She's not in good shape."

"I understand. She's been missing for three weeks or so. Please, let me see her." Ciaran's voice broke as he spoke. Then brushing past the doctor, he moved to the curtain, stopping for a moment to calm himself, before he brushed the curtain aside and entered.

He didn't see the nurses and physicians working around MaKenna. Didn't see the lab tech come in and draw blood. He didn't see the ventilator she was on, the IV lines running to her arm, the leads from the cardiac monitor. All he saw was that she was there and alive.

The head nurse took a look at him, opened her mouth, and then didn't speak as the physician shook his head.

He was finally able to move to the bedside, his eyes fastened on her face. He reached out to grasp her hand, and as he touched her cold flesh, tears streamed down his face. He didn't hear the words spoken to him as he reached to trace her face.

He finally turned as a hand was laid on his shoulder and he recognized the physician standing there.

"Dan?"

"Ciaran? This is your wife? I didn't know you had married."

"It's a long story, Dan. She was abducted three weeks or so. Tell me she'll be all right."

"There are a lot of things going on with her, Ciaran. We need to talk but first we have to stabilize her more and then move her to an ICU bed." Dan watched with concern the fragility he saw in his friend. "Are you okay?"

Ciaran's one shoulder raised and lowered in a half-hearted shrug. "I have MaKenna back. That's what counts."

"Not totally. You need your strength too, if you're to get through this." Dan turned for a moment, then at a movement from

Ciaran, turned back, catching his friend as he collapsed, eyes rolling back.

Quick movement had Ciaran on a stretcher in another cubicle. Dan was torn. He needed to be both of them. A quick examination and he was giving orders to the nurses, before moving back to stand and stare at Ciaran.

"His parents are here?"

The nurse, Susan, nodded. "They are. MaKenna, is it? Her mother's here as well. Angus said Beth and Makenna's brother are on their way."

"Do they have someone with them?" He shot a look back at the closed entry door.

"They do. Paul's out there as well as some of the deacons from church."

"Good. Now, about MaKenna. I'm worried about her. There's hypothermia in play there."

☆ ☆ ☆ ☆ ☆

Art finally found his way to the hospital and, after asking for a room number, made his way to Ciaran's room. He stood for a moment in the doorway, his eyes searching the dim room. It was after midnight but he had come to check on his friend. He had bypassed the waiting room, knowing the family would be there.

He approached the bed and stood for a moment watching as Ciaran stirred.

"Art?" Ciaran blinked at him before looking around. "Where am I?"

"In the hospital, friend. You collapsed downstairs."

"I did? I don't remember." He pushed himself up in the bed, a tired sigh coming from him. "What do you have for news? Have you found MaKenna yet?"

"You really don't remember?" Art stared at him for a moment.

"Remember what? The last thing I remember is that Dad and I were pouring over maps in the kitchen. Why am I here?" He pushed at the blanket and fumbled as he tried to find the latch for the bedside.

Art sighed, then reached to pull a chair up. It was going to be a long conversation, and he had no idea how he would keep Ciaran from leaving his bed to find the ICU unit.

"You don't remember me calling you this morning? Or our conversation? Or why you're here?"

Ciaran shook his head. "No, I don't. Should I?"

"You should. What I'm about to tell you means you need to stay right here. We found MaKenna." He watched as Ciaran struggled to once more realize that his wife had been found. "She's here in an ICU bed and no, you can't go to her. Not yet." He reached to lay a hand on Ciaran's arm. "The doctor said in the morning, you'll be able to. He was concerned that you collapsed."

"Of course I collapsed. Who wouldn't with that news?" He struggled to sit upright, then slumped back as the room swirled around him. "Not a good idea."

"No, that wasn't. That's why you need to wait."

"How is she?" The desperation in his voice pulled at Art.

"She's in rough shape, Ciaran. Hypothermia. Malnutrion. Weight loss. Pneumonia, they think. She wasn't abused or beaten." He paused, struggling once more to understand the whys and how to explain what he did and didn't know to his friend. "We have no idea who it was. Not yet. The doctor thinks it's be a couple of days before she's awake enough to talk to but even then she might not know anything."

"Where'd you find her?"

"In an old abandoned building in the downtown area. She was in a room someone had built just for her. No windows. It looks as if she'd been there for at least two weeks."

"So they moved her from the first building we looked at?"

Art shook his heard. "Other than her shoe, there was no evidence she was there for any length of time."

Ciaran's head went back as his eyes slid closed. "What kind of monster does this?"

"One we will find, I promise you that."

"What about her father?"

"No sign of him, but I'm sure he's still around. I've posted officers at her door and at yours. Listen, I need to run. I'm heading home for a few hours of sleep, but I just wanted to talk to you."

"Thanks, Art. Find out when I can get out of here." Ciaran drifted off to sleep before his friend had reached the door.

Art gave a low laugh and a wave as he left the room. He stopped, his face sobering. Yes, they had found MaKenna but who had taken her and how safe was she really?

★ ★ ★ ★ ★

Ciaran drew a deep breath, then stepped into the room where MaKenna lay. Once more he only had eyes for her face, not for any of the equipment surrounding her. He didn't remember doing the same thing less that twenty-four hours previously but he had.

He stood, his hand on her cheek, before he reached to brush a kiss on her forehead. He straightened up, his heart hurting at how she looked, her hair matted and dirty, her face pale and thin, scratches and bruises on her arms. He finally looked up, taking in the equipment around her bed, knowing it was necessary, but hating that it was. He had been warned that he only had a limited time with her for now. He studied her face again, seeing the ravages her ordeal had placed there. He didn't know if she'd ever get past them but his prayer was that she would. If he had to, he'd move towns with her and start up all over again. Whatever it took, that became the chant within him. Thank you, Lord. You brought her back to me. Now, please, dear Lord, heal her. Let her have that touch on the garment that heals.

He looked back as the nurse touched his arm. He nodded, taking one last look at his wife and dropping another kiss on her face. He looked back again from the doorway, then straightened, a resolve hardening in his heart. He would find whoever it was, by legal means or not. They would be brought to justice.

He heard footsteps approaching and looked up to see his father and Riordan walking towards him.

"How is she, son?" Angus nodded towards the door.

"She's still out of it. The nurse said she's doing as well as they could expect right now. Who did this, Dad?"

Angus shook his head. "I don't know, son, but we'll find him."

"That's right, we will. Right now, I need to go….. I need to go somewhere but I can't remember just where." Ciaran looked around, confusion on his face.

Riordan shook his head at Angus. This was to be expected, his silence said.

"Come on, Ciaran. Let's head for the cafeteria. You need to eat." His father reached for his arm.

"No, I don't need to eat." He wrenched his arm from his father's loose grasp.

"Yes, you do. If you don't, you'll collapse again like yesterday. And that won't help MaKenna or help you find whoever it is that did this."

Seated in the cafeteria, a plate of toast in front of him, Ciaran sank his head into his hands. The two men with him shared another look. How did they reach him?

"Ciaran, what about your work for tomorrow?"

Ciaran raised blood-shot eyes. "I talked to the homeowner this morning and explained. It's actually Paul's mother. She said to take what time I needed and come back. She's fine with it. I left a mess there on Friday."

"It's been cleaned up. Paul and some friends from church looked after it. He said you'd made good progress in the kitchen, enough that his Mom can survive. If anything, she'll go stay with him."

"Thanks for that, Dad. Now what?"

"Now what is that you eat that." Angus pointed at the toast. "We're not to allow you back to the ICU unit unless you've eaten."

"Yeah? Who says?"

"Your Mom. And Sarah." Angus gave a grin at the look on Ciaran's face. "Eat, son. You can't argue with a mother."

Riordan was watching the two men but movement behind them caught his attention and he looked past them. A frown covered his face. He knew that face of the man back there, but for now he couldn't put a name to it. He just knew the man wasn't there for himself. His eyes had been too focused on Ciaran. He pulled out his phone, snapping a quick photo, and then sending it on to Art with a quick text.

Art turned from the elevator in the hospital and headed for where the men sat. His eyes searched the room and found the man Riordan had just seen watching them leaving the room. Art turned, watching as he headed for the exit. He would ensure that the officers on duty at MaKenna's door had a copy of that photo.

He slid into a chair beside Riordan, greeting the three men, his eyes centred on Ciaran.

"How's MaKenna this morning?"

Ciaran looked up from where he was pushing crumbs around on his plate with one finger. "I've been in to see her. About the same, I think the nurse said. Her mother and

Riordan are going in shortly. Riordan, you should likely head up there and meet your mother.”

Riordan nodded and rose, his glance taking in the three men and then stopping at Art. Art nodded and Riordan drew a deep breath. There was some kind of word, but he wouldn’t be here to find out what. Art, he knew, would catch up with him later.

Art drew a deep breath, then rose and headed to buy them all a fresh round of coffee. His eyes searched the room as he returned to the table, the tray balanced in his hand, stepping sideways to avoid a toddler heading for the food, giving a quick grin to the little girl’s mother as she mouthed an apology. He didn’t see anyone that raised concern, but someone was there, he knew.

“Art, what news do you have?” Angus spoke for them both.

“Not a lot, yet. I haven’t been to the office this morning to speak with the team, but they’ve been giving updates through the night.” He paused to sip at the hot coffee, grimacing at the bitterness. “You would think they could make better coffee than this. Anyway, from what we’ve been able to determine, MaKenna was held there for most of the time. I won’t go into details yet as to what it was like. She may or may not remember but it's part of the investigation that we want to keep quiet."

"We understand that. But how did you find her?"

"By fluke, some would say. I like to think by divine intervention. A neighbour saw people going in and out of a supposedly empty building and called the building supervisor ten days ago. He did nothing, not wanting to get involved with the type of people who use empty buildings. The man finally called in to us late Friday afternoon. We obtained a search warrant and went in. We've had to wait for an amended search warrant to go back in, but we had that yesterday afternoon. We're working through that building, talking to neighbours, that kind of stuff. Lots of legwork, dead ends and frustration." He paused, his eyes searching Ciaran's face. "But we have MaKenna back."

"We do, and I can't thank you enough." Ciaran shoved his cup back and made to stand.

"Before you go, son, let's spend some time in prayer." Angus reached for his son, laying his hand on Ciaran's arm. "There's still a lot of work for Art and he needs our

help in whatever way we can give it. Your
lady needs to heal and so do you. Sit, son."
He waited until Ciaran had slid back into his
chair. "We're not giving up. We'll continue
to work with what we can. Right now, your
job is to be by MaKenna and help her to heal.
That and keep working. Your Mom and hers
will help."

"Dad, I think we need to see if we can
bring Emma in. That may reach her where
nothing else can."

Art nodded. "Leave that with me. I'll
get her in, somehow, even if I have to
smuggle her in. Didn't you say she had been
approved as a therapy dog?" When Ciaran
nodded, he continued. "Then, that's how we
do it. Your wife needs a visit from a therapy
dog. I'll get you approved quick to be her
handler. Then they can't say anything."

"How?"

"Paul's one of the evaluators. He's
seen you with her. That helps."

Ciaran paced the waiting room, ready
to go back in to see his wife, but knowing he
had to wait. He wasn't good at waiting. He
paused at the window, his hand resting on the
window pane, watching the rain run down it
in rivulets. This was not how he had planned
to spend this weekend. He had planned to

take MaKenna somewhere really nice for the weekend, treat her to some lovely romantic dinners and quiet walks in some parks somewhere, just to spoil her. Instead, he was standing here and she was laying in a room down the hall, not aware of anyone around her. Lord, when? When will it end?

He felt someone stop beside and caught Riordan's reflection in the window beside him. They stood for a while, lost in their thoughts, before Ciaran spoke.

"Not giving me platitudes, words, what have you, Riordan?"

"Nope. I'd have to give them to myself, and I've learned over the years that sometimes all a person needs is someone to stand beside them, in silence, sharing their burden. Someone to stand in the gap, as we say."

Ciaran nodded. "Thanks. I've had many people doing just that. Saying things, who have no idea what it's been like."

"People try, Ciaran. They feel like they have to say something." Riordan turned enough that he could scan the waiting room before turning back to Ciaran. "What did Art have to say?"

"Not much. He thinks she was there most of the time, but he can't say much of what it was like." He sighed, wanting the details but not wanting them. "How's your mom?"

"Hanging in there. Your mom is heading back to their place with her. They'll be back later today. Beth has headed out somewhere as well."

"Dad?"

Riordan gave a low laugh. "Your dad is a real character, you know that. He made sure the ladies were taken care, made sure I was staying, then headed out himself. He said he had to leave tonight to travel for another court case."

Ciaran nodded. "He does. He doesn't want to but he doesn't have much choice. He thinks he'll be back Tuesday night, late."

Nodding, Riordan turned so his back leaned against the window. "I have to head back tomorrow. I have some meetings I can't miss, that I've worked to set up. I wish I could stay longer."

"MaKenna would understand Riordan. Just watch your back. I'm afraid they might come after you to get to MaKenna. She's said that as well. She's worried about you."

Riordan shook his head. "Somehow, I don't think they will. They'll come after who's the nearest and dearest to her. That's you. Dad won't do that to me. He told me once he won't fight me, that if I wanted to walk away, just to do that. That's about all I was worth any way."

Ciaran tilted his head to study the man standing beside. "Your father really is a piece of work. He's trying to destroy three lives." He held up a hand as Riordan went to protest. "He's done that, and right now he's out there somewhere, still doing that. My gut instinct says that he's behind all this, that he was behind your uncle's death. I just can't prove it."

Riordan dropped his head until his chin rested on his chest. He was exhausted, his mind tired and foggy. He straightened up. "They'll be letting you back in shortly, Ciaran. I'm heading out. Call me if you need me." He hesitated as he reached into his pocket and pulled out his keys. "I'll try and get back by Thursday."

Ciaran reached to hug his brother-in-law. "Call me when you get home. I want to know you're safe."

Riordan nodded, walking away rapidly so Ciaran didn't see the tears in his eyes.

Ciaran watched him go, then turned as he heard his name called. Art stood there. His eyes studied Ciaran before he pointed at some chairs.

Ciaran sighed, not wanting to hear any more details or failures, but knowing he needed to.

"Art?"

"Nothing new, Ciaran. I just needed to come and sit with you for a while, just as a friend. You'll never know what your example and witness have meant to me." Art sat, his head going back as his eyes closed, fatigue, no, deep-rooted exhaustion evident.

"How so?" Ciaran was curious. Right now, he felt like he was the worst example.

"Even in the midst of all this, when you had no idea if you would see MaKenna again, your faith stayed true. I know it was shaken, and still is, but it has led me back to my roots." He groaned as his phone chimed. "I wish I could just shut this off for a whole day and just sleep." He read the text, then sent a reply. "They found some evidence they feel is good that will lead to who took her. Your brother-in-law saw one of the men this morning and got his picture. The patrol officers have addressed it."

Ciaran stared at him. "I didn't know that he had."

"He did. He was sitting behind you and your Dad this morning in the cafeteria."

Ciaran sat back, his mind whirling that evil had been that close to him and he didn't even know it.

Chapter 13

$\mathscr{M}$aKenna saw the shadows surrounding her and turned, trying to find the exit, the way that would lead her out of this nightmare. She couldn't see it. She could hear the footsteps of the man coming towards her again and again, following her wherever she went. She just couldn't get away from him. She turned and fought, fought against the hands holding her hands, fought whatever it was that was choking her, trying to reach out past the darkness to where she knew it was light. She was losing the battle and she slipped further into the darkness.

The doctor and nurses in her ICU room fought to bring her back. Someone, somehow, had gotten to her, turning off all the monitors and the ventilator, pulling out the IV's running to her veins with life-saving drugs and fluids. The doctor finally stepped back, his arm swiping away the sweat on his forehead, as he studied the monitors and then MaKenna.

"There. We did it, team. She's back. That was too close. How'd that happen?" His eyes assessed the nurses and techs in the room.

"We have no idea, Dr. Thomas. We heard the monitors and ran for her. By that time, whoever it was had disappeared. The officer at the door was on the floor unconscious. Dr. Andrews is looking after him but thinks he may have been drugged. And the security system blanked out for about five minutes."

"Very handy." He stepped back to the bed, stethoscope to his ears and MaKenna's chest as he listened, then reached for her wrist for her pulse. "I want the cardiologist on call in today. I don't like the sounds of her heart. With what she went through and the hypothermia, there may be damage we need to look at." He turned keen eyes on the head nurse, Lee, and nodded. "Where's her husband?"

"Glued to the wall outside. We can't get him to move from there."

"All right. Get him in here. I understand they want to bring in her dog? Let them. That may reach her where nothing else will. If I need to sign off on that, let me know." He assessed MaKenna again. "Any word if they found out who did this?"

"Not that I've heard. I know Art. He's my cousin. He can't say anything but his silence when I asked said it all."

Dr. Thomas nodded, then turned as Ciaran stood hesitantly in the doorway. "Get in here to your wife, young man. We had a bit of a set back as you know, but she's still with us."

Ciaran nodded, his eyes on MaKenna, as he moved forward to stand beside her, his hand reached to grasp hers.

Dr. Thomas stood back, his eyes assessing Ciaran, then frowning as he turned to read the monitors. He kept watching, then turned to Lee. "Let him stay in here as long as he wants. Her vitals have improved now that he's here."

Lee had noted that and then nodded. "We will. I know Art will be putting more security in place."

Dr. Thomas nodded, then spoke. "My brother has a security team. Call him and ask him to contact Art and volunteer his services. That will help. We need to keep her safe and obviously we can't."

MaKenna stirred, her eyes flickering open and closed. She tried to swallow and had difficulty doing that. She couldn't lick her lips that felt dry and sore. She moved, pain in her joints preventing from moving too much.

Her eyes finally stayed open, and she stared around through pain-filled eyes. Where was she? Her head turned, her eyes taking in the monitors and then hearing the hiss of the ventilator, realized she wasn't breathing on her own. Her hand reached to pull the tube and another hand on hers stopped the movement. She stared at the window for a moment, seeing the darkness outside before turning to face who it was that stood beside her.

Ciaran watched as she roused, his hand on hers. She frowned as she saw him, not recognizing him before her eyes slid shut and she slept again. Ciaran sighed, then dropped a kiss on her forehead. He had been warned this may be the case. He had prayed that she would recognize him as soon as she awoke. He turned as he heard the door swish open and quick rubber-soled shoes squeaking across the floor.

Lee stood for a moment, assessing Ciaran, and then turning to the monitors.

"There's been a change, Ciaran?" She reached to check the flow of the IV fluid.

He nodded, not able to speak for a moment. "She was just awake. She tried to pull the ventilator out."

Lee turned to him, surprise on her face. "We didn't expect her to be awake for at least another day or two, not after that scare the other day." She turned to leave. "I'll be right back. Dr. Thomas will want to know. We can likely put her on oxygen now."

MaKenna's eyes opened during the early morning hours, this time staying open. She felt more alert. She reached for her face, feeling just the nasal prongs for the oxygen. Turning her head slightly, she stared at the monitors for a moment, then around the room, finally resting at the chair pulled tight to the side of the bed and the man sleeping there, his head back, one hand tucked up on his chest, the other holding her hand tight. She frowned for a moment. Who was he? She felt like she should know him.

Memories filtered through, bits and pieces, until she realized that it was Ciaran. She sighed softly, her eyes on his, not wanting to wake him. She moved her hand, and his tightened on hers, his eyes slowly opening.

Ciaran awoke slowly, feeling MaKenna's hand moving under his. He looked up and found her eyes on him, recognition dawning in hers.

"You're back, love." He stood, carefully moving to drop a kiss on her cheek.

"Ciaran?" Her voice was hoarse and she had to swallowing order to speak. "What happened?"

"You had an adventure without me, love, but you came back to me." He reached to brush her hair back from her face. Her mother had been adamant that she had to wash it, that it would make her daughter feel better, and with the nurse's help, had managed just that.

"I did? I don't remember." She moved restlessly, almost in fear. "Don't let him hurt me again, Ciaran."

"Who, love? Don't let who hurt you?"

"I don't know. I just know that he wanted to kill me, didn't want me to live. I couldn't tell him what he wanted to know, and he left me by myself."

"Ssh, love. None of that now. Just rest. No one can get to you. We have someone at the door and I'm right here."

MaKenna yawned, then gave a small smile. "Don't leave me, Ciaran. I can't do that again." She slept.

Ciaran stood for a while, his hand on her cheek, his hand on hers, before he straightened up and moved way, anger coursing through him. Art had been right, then. Whoever it was had planned that MaKenna not come back to them, that she not live. What was it that he wanted? Ciaran couldn't think of anything other than the two keys and those had been dealt with.

Late that afternoon, Art stood beside her bedside, notepad in hand, pen posed to write, watching as MaKenna lay there, her eyes on Ciaran, as she tried to compose her thoughts. She looks some better, he thought, but she has a ways to go yet. He knew there was still concerns about her heart, that there may have been damage from what she went through, but she was moving to a private room the next day. That would make it easier for security to be in place. He was thankful that Dr. Thomas' brother had stepped in.

"MaKenna, tell me what happened. We didn't find much evidence, other than some scuff marks in the sawdust on the porch."

She nodded, her eyes coming to meet his. "I can't remember everything. I think I'm blocking out portions of it. Dr. Thomas said I would. I'll tell you what I remember, as I remember it, then sign it as a statement. Can we do that?"

Art nodded. "We can. Let me set up a recording device. Then I'll have it transcribed for you. There, we're set. You talk. When you're done, I'll shut it off and then question you on the points I need clarification on."

She nodded, waited for him to indicate she could speak, then reached for the glass of water Ciaran held. She looked up at him, seeing the shadows in his eyes.

She started to speak, giving the date and time and her full name, along with the words that she was giving her statement freely and without coercion.

"I was taken from the house my husband is renovating. I am helping him, not going back to my work as a medical office assistant. I was working on the porch, starting to tidy it up, when a man approached me from behind, wrapping an arm around me, trapping mine, and then a hand over my mouth. He carried me to a van, where another man was waiting. I was blindfolded, bound and gagged. I fought them as best as I could. I tried to scream but couldn't get any sound out. I was thrown into the back of the van and they drove around for a while. I know they talked but it was too low to hear anything. I was walked into a building. It was smelly, and dirty, and old. I couldn't tell what kind of building. I was then shoved into a room and left there. There were no windows.

"Once a day, they brought in two bottles of water and one sandwich. When they would come in, they would question me as to where it was. I'd tell them I had no idea what "it" was. They finally left me alone. I have no idea how long for.

"I gave up, I think. I just knew they wouldn't come back and I wouldn't be found." She bit her lip at this point as she paused to control her emotions, her hand tightening to a death grip on Ciaran's. "I just laid down and went to sleep. I was so cold, just not thirsty or hungry anymore. And that's about it, until I woke up here. I have no idea how long it was. There were no windows in the room. The only way I could see it was daytime was when light would come in faintly around the door. I tried to get out the door but couldn't."

Art nodded as he clicked off the recorder, knowing he had gotten as much from her as he could. "That's good, MaKenna. Now, any scents, smells, sounds that you recognized?"

She shook her head. "I was too scared to even think about something like that. I was afraid they would kill me that first day."

He nodded again as he pocketed his notepad, pen and recorder. "If you think of anything, call me. Just so you know, we did go through the building. We have some evidence that we're working through. And we have arrested one man involved. He's not talking yet and has refused a lawyer."

Ciaran walked him out, stopping in the doorway where he could watch MaKenna. "Any other news, Art?"

"Not that I can share. We're getting close, Ciaran. Your job is to spend time helping your wife heal. In a way, healing from what she went through may be easier. She won't be haunted by the faces of the men, won't be looking for them wherever she goes. On the other hand, with not knowing what they look like, she'll suspect everyone. Has your Dad found out anything more?"

Ciaran shook his head. "He's been away on a court case. He said he's tracking financials for someone involved, but won't say who or why."

Art nodded. "I'll keep in touch. Listen, I have to be away for a few days. A family commitment I can't get out of. Tony Brown will be working on this while I'm away. Contact him if you need anything. Here's his card."

"Thanks, Art, but it won't be the same."

"No, it won't. Take care, my friend."

Ciaran watched him walk away and then turned to reenter the room, stopping as he felt eyes on him. He spun, not seeing anyone other than medical staff. He frowned, not liking that idea at all. He would take MaKenna home as soon as he could.

MaKenna was sleeping again, turned on her side, her hand tucked under her cheek. He stood for a moment, then dropped a kiss on her hair, turning to find the chair that he had been sitting in. He too slept.

MaKenna finally sat in her own living room three days later, Emma wrapped in her arms, the dog's tongue licking as fast as she could at any exposed flesh. She sank back, exhausted. Ciaran stood for a moment, then headed to get her a cup of tea, knowing that's what she would want.

He sat beside her, then pulled both MaKenna and Emma into his arms, tears on his cheeks as he did so.

"Need anything else, love?" He felt the head shake. "I'm so glad you're home."

"Me, too. I didn't think I'd get out so soon, though."

"You amazed the doctors, love. They really expected you'd be needing a lot more care than you do. We just need to get your strength back."

She nodded, then spoke. "I need to talk to Paul, though, Ciaran. I need to go over what happened and how God locked after me and I need to do that with someone's that's not family."

"I think it's wise. I'll call him later. Right now, I just want to sit and hold my girl." A low woof caused them to laugh. "All right, Emma. Hold both my girls."

Chapter 14

Four weeks later, Ciaran looked both ways before he ran across the street towards the town hall. He had paperwork to file and wanted to get home to MaKenna. She had healed physically and was working through the emotional trauma, he knew, meeting weekly with their pastor.

Art had told him the day before that the case was growing cold, that there had been no new leads in either her abduction or the discovery of her uncle's skeleton. He hated to hear that but knew it was true. His father hadn't found any other information that would help. MaKenna's father was still on the run, and they weren't sure yet where he was.

He turned in his paperwork, then stood for a moment on the sidewalk, staring at the stores in front of him. He walked quickly towards one, made his purchase, and then headed back towards his truck. He had to stop on the way home to pick up their dinner, and he knew it was waiting for him at their local diner.

He stopped, his eyes searching the area around him before he slid from the truck. He didn't hear the squealing of tires that came towards him until someone yelled. He jumped back as the van sped by, just missing him. He shook his head and looked up as the men in the parking lot ran towards him, one with a phone out.

"Are you okay?" The first man searched him over.

"I am. Did you get a plate number?"

"Only a partial." The man looked in the direction the van had gone. "He was aiming right for you."

"I didn't see him. Thanks." Ciaran groaned. "I guess that means my wife's supper will be late."

"Pardon?"

"I was here to pick up supper for my wife and I. Guess that's not happening."

"Ciaran, just come in when you're done and I'll have a fresh order for you." Dave from the diner spoke behind him.

"Thanks, Dave. Hopefully it won't be long." Ciaran looked up as he heard the patrol car pull in. "At least it didn't take long for them to get here."

After giving his statement and asking that Art be advised, Ciaran headed into the diner and grabbed their meal, his eyes watchful.

MaKenna watched him as he moved around the house, knowing something had happened and waiting for him to speak. When he hadn't by bedtime, she turned to him.

"What happened today, hon?"

He turned. "Someone tried to run me down today. No, I don't think it's related to what's going on. Just some fluke."

She reached to hug him as he folded her close in his arms. "You're not hurt? Thank God."

☆ ☆ ☆ ☆ ☆

The next day, Ciaran walked towards the house he was renovating, stopping as he saw the destruction outside of the house. His heart sank at the destroyed stacks of lumber. He ran for the door, finding it still locked, and opened it to run inside. Everything inside was how he had left it. Now, who would have done that? He pulled out his phone, made the calls he needed to, then sat on the porch steps, chin in his hands as he waited.

Art stood for a moment staring at the ruined lumber, then at Ciaran, who watched him from where he sat on the front steps of the house.

"Somebody not happy with you?" Art sat beside him.

"I have no idea. It was fine when I left yesterday. I almost get run down getting dinner last night. Now this?" He turned his head to stare at Art. "You tell me. Is it related to what we're going through?"

"I have no idea. We couldn't find the van. We just didn't have enough information to do that, but we'll still work it. How's MaKenna?"

"She still struggles at times. She's wanting to come work with me, but the fear is there, keeping her from doing just that. She spends a lot of time with her mom and mine. Say, what happened to Dr. Stirling?"

"He and his wife moved to the city. They felt it safer. He didn't see who hit him or dragged him from his office, but the impression he got is similar to what you and MaKenna have been describing. So it's likely the same group, though why, we don't know. MaKenna's missed at that office, you know?"

"I know. Anna's been in touch." Ciaran's voice died away as he said that. "What do you know about Anna?"

"What do you mean?" Art was interested to hear where Ciaran was going with that.

"She had every opportunity to do what happened at the office with an accomplice. Does she have a husband, boyfriend, friend, brother who would help?"

"We've given her a cursory look, but the team's going back through everyone and pulling out everything they can find on them." Art stood. "I have to get back to the office. Stay safe, friend, and keep your lady safe."

"I will and thanks." Ciaran watched him pull away. He sighed. The patrol officer had been and taken his statement, the new lumber was here, and he needed to get to work. He squinted at the sun. Still half a day to go. He sighed and stood. Work was not going to get done while he sat there.

MaKenna turned from the stove as he walked in the back door that night, his feet dragging from fatigue.

"Ciaran?"

He shook his head. "After dinner, love. I'll talk then. Do I have time to clean up?"

"You do. Don't forget we're supposed to meet your parents for coffee later."

He groaned. "I had. Can you call them and put it off? I'm just not up to it tonight."

"I can, but you have to promise to talk to me after."

He dropped a kiss on her upturned face and just held her for a few minutes before heading off to shower and change.

She watched him walk away, knowing something had happened that day. She sighed. She looked over at the counter, at the envelope laying there that she hadn't opened. It seemed they both had things to talk about that night.

Ciaran drew MaKenna into his arms on the couch later that night. "So, how was your day?"

"You first. What happened at work?"

"I had a bunch of lumber destroyed outside and had to replace it. Art stopped by and we talked for a bit. Nothing new to report."

She nodded, then pointed at the envelope. "That came today."

"That envelope? What about it?"

"It matches the other ones I got." She shuddered even as she remembered them. "He's still watching us, Ciaran. When will it end?"

Ciaran reached for the envelope and opened it, dropping out pictures of the two of them going about their life. His hand froze as he saw the last one, with an X through the both of them. "I don't like this, MaKenna."

She snorted. "Now, why would I think you would? I don't either. We need to end this somehow, Ciaran. We have a right to live our lives in peace. Where is God in this?" She stood, glaring at him, hands on her hips. "Why is He letting this continue?"

"So, what do we do?"

She paced, her head bent, arms wrapped around her. Ciaran sat and watched her, his arm around Emma who sat tight to him, her brown eyes watching MaKenna.

"We need to come up with some kind of plan. Do you think there's anything left in my house that we didn't find?"

He shrugged. "We never did go over it all the way, did we? Is there an attic? I never looked."

"There is. You go in through a crawl space in the garage. There is flooring down up there. I never went up after I peeked the first time."

"We'll check it out on Saturday. Then look back through the house. Have you decided what you want to do with it?"

She shrugged. "I have no idea. I need to decide soon." She sighed as she sank back down on the couch. "I think I'll sell it. I need to get rid of it."

"That's sounds okay." He rose and headed for the kitchen. "Let's plan on that. Do we have any ice cream left?"

"Ice cream? How can you eat after this?"

He peeked back around the door. "I don't know. It's what I sometimes do when I'm stressed. Do you want some?"

"No!"

Art tracked Ciaran down the next day and stood for a moment watching him work. Then he spoke, startling Ciaran.

"Ciaran, got a moment?"

Ciaran turned for a moment. "Sure. Just let me finish this. It won't take long."

Five minutes later, he turned to Art, puzzled that he had tracked him down again.

"What did you want?"

"MaKenna brought in that envelope. Were you planning on calling me?"

Ciaran shrugged. "Likely, but I don't know for sure. This is just so weird, Art. We don't hear from them for weeks, and they start up again."

"It is strange, but I wonder…." Art's voice died away. "Have you heard anything from her father?"

Ciaran shook his head. "Not a word. None of us have. Why?"

"It just we're still hearing rumours about what he was mixed up in years ago. That building you found with the counterfeiting and drug making equipment? I've heard he was the one who ran it."

Ciaran shrugged. "Doesn't surprise me, but what has that to do with what we're dealing with now?"

"Just listen for a moment. Say, he had lots of money not circulated and Timothy took it and hid it. He'd been trying to find it now that we've found Timothy. He'd think there would have been something on the body to say where it was hidden."

Ciaran slumped back against the wall, rubbing the back of his neck. "That makes sense, but we never found anything at all. Why would he think that?"

Art shrugged. "Who knows?"

"We need to end this, Art. MaKenna can't completely heal or go on with her life if this continues."

"I know that, Ciaran. Believe me, I wish I could end this. The photos don't help push the case forward."

"I didn't think they would. Look, I'm running behind today. Can we talk later?"

Art nodded and then left, leaving Ciaran staring after him, pulling out his phone to scan the text message that had arrived. His face whitened as he read it, before he pocketed his phone. He knew MaKenna was safe, but the threats were growing. He hadn't told Art that he was getting more and more of them, each one worse than the one before it.

He stopped, realizing that he was trying to do it in his own strength and that didn't cut it as his father would say. He prayed, leaving it with God, and walking back to his work. Now, what, he thought? This can't go on for much longer. MaKenna needed it to end.

"Are you sure this is the only way into the attic?" Ciaran stood on the stepladder in the garage and looked back down at MaKenna.

She grinned up at him. "It's the only one I know of but there might be more. You can look around when you're up there."

"I guess that means you're not coming up?" He grinned back down at her as he headed through the trapdoor, switching on the powerful flashlight he had brought with him. "Did you know there are lights up here?"

"No, I didn't." She waited, listening to him move around before she got brave enough to climb the ladder and stick her head through the opening. "Found anything yet?"

"Yes, there's is a trap door to the house, but it's sealed shut." He turned on his knees, looking around with a frown in place. "This doesn't make sense, MaKenna. Why seal up an entrance from the house?"

"Will we have to pull up the flooring?"

He shook his head. "This is at least thirty years old and doesn't look like it's been disturbed since it was put down. Now, what is that?" He crawled across the floor, the light shining on a metal box under one of the eaves. He pulled it forward, finding it heavy. "If you'll go back down, I'll hand you the light and then pull this down."

MaKenna watched as he tugged the heavy metal box down the ladder and then lifted it to a work bench.

"Ciaran?"

"I know, MaKenna. It could be what we're looking for, or it could be nothing." He looked around the garage. "Did you put the work bench in place?"

"No. It was already here as were the tools. Why?" She stared around. "You're thinking something is hidden in here."

He nodded as he brushed dust and cobwebs off of himself. "The house has been searched. We haven't looked out here."

"Someone went to a lot of work to hide this." Ciaran carefully lifted the lid and laid it on the bench. "Do you have your phone on you?"

"I do. Oh, you want pictures."

He nodded. "We'll need pictures. I'm sure we'll have to turn this over to Art."

They went page by page through the papers. It was what Ciaran had expected to find, names, dates, lists of payments, lists where counterfeit money had been passed, names of drug dealers.

"This is going to create a lot of work for Art and his gang." Ciaran looked around as he stuffed everything back in the box and put the lid back on. "Let's look around in here first before we leave."

Ciaran finally stepped back. "I don't see anything. I'd need to rip out the workbench thought to make sure."

MaKenna handed him the pry bar she was holding. "Go for it. We might as well tear everything out now that we started. Then we won't have to return."

He laughed as she said, but realized the truth in her words. Once they left today, she wouldn't be back, he knew. This was it.

Moving the heavy bench forward sent screeching and scraping sounds through the garage. MaKenna's hands went to her ears as she stepped backwards.

Ciaran stopped, his chest heaving with the exertion. "I can get in there now. Where's the flashlight?"

He shone it behind the bench. "There is something back here, another recess. A small one." He struggled to reach it, finally moving the bench back a bit more, to pull out another box. "These people liked their boxes, didn't they? Now, let me check. That's seems to be it. Let me move the bench back, and then we'll take a look at that."

MaKenna reached for the box, studying, a memory tickling at the edge of her thoughts. "This was my uncle's, Ciaran. I remember seeing in a couple of times when we visited him."

Ciaran searched her face, then reached for her hands to set the box down. "Let's seen what's inside, shall we?"

She drew a deep breath, knowing that when it was opened, there would be no going back. She nodded to him, her eyes on his.

Ciaran worked the lid off the small box, carefully setting it down. "There's another key, love. Smaller than the ones we found. And a note."

She shivered suddenly, feeling evil approaching. She turned, finding a cardboard box and handing it to Ciaran. "Can we pack everything in this and take it with us? We need to leave and leave now."

Ciaran shot her a glance and then nodded. "We can do that, love. Head back into the house. I'm right behind you." He searched the garage and didn't see anything else they needed. The house echoed back their footsteps, MaKenna and their mothers having packed up everything and moves it to Ciaran's.

"Do you need any more time here, love?" Ciaran's arms came around her.

"I don't think so, sweetheart. I'm ready to leave and go on with the next step in our lives. I couldn't stay here anyway."

"No, I don't think you could. The shelves look good, though. Have you talked to a realtor?"

She nodded. "The sign goes up tomorrow. Hopefully it sells quickly. I need to be done with it."

Chapter 15

$\mathcal{A}$rt stared at the paperwork spread out on Ciaran's dining room table and listened to the quiet conversation between Ciaran and Angus. MaKenna was in the kitchen. He could hear the quiet sounds of water running, the coffee pot perking, the whistling of a boiled kettle quickly stopped, the click of mugs set on a tray, the metal clinks of spoons. He stepped to the kitchen and stopped for a moment, just watching her.

"Art? Are you okay?" MaKenna's concern for him came through.

"I am. Thanks, MaKenna. Now what can it do for you?"

"You can take that tray through to the dining room. I'm right behind you with this plate of sandwiches."

"Sandwiches? What? You think we haven't eaten?"

She laughed at his cocky grin. "I know you have, but I also know that you are likely hungry again. Ciaran always needs something before he retires." She paused for a moment. "Before we go in, where does the investigation really stand?"

"It's coming slowly, MaKenna. We're working it through, but we've had other cases we've had to tackle. I'm sorry."

"That's okay. It's what I expected. Until something happens again, we get put on the back burner."

She brushed past him, but he saw the sorrow in her eyes. Yes, he definitely needed to solve this and soon.

Art stood listening to Angus, his eyes on the paper.

"You found this where, Ciaran?"

"In a cavity behind the workbench. The bench hadn't been moved in a long time. The other box we found in the attic." Ciaran's eyes met MaKenna.

"That's interesting. Now this key, what does it unlock?"

"I think we need to look outside the house and property again." Angus reached for it and studied it. "It's to an old locked box, I would say, but where it would be, I have no idea."

Art nodded. "That is a problem." He stopped as MaKenna reached for the key.

"I have an idea where the box is." She reached for her phone. "Riordan, does Mom still have those boxes of Uncle Timothy's?"

"As far as I know, she does. We've cleaned out the house and rented it. I think she took everything and put it into storage there. I know I don't have anything of his. Why?"

"Just a thought. I'll talk to her tomorrow."

"Okay. Do I need to come over there?"

"I don't think so. I'll call you again tomorrow."

She shared a look with Ciaran. "Mom still has boxes of things that were Uncle Timothy's. Dad wanted to through them out but for some reason backed off when Mom refused. Riordan says there is a storage unit here somewhere. I'll talk to her in the morning and find out where."

Ciaran wrapped an arm around her. "Talk to her and get the key. Tomorrow's Friday. We'll look through the boxes on Saturday. You're free, Dad?"

Angus shook his head. "Unfortunately, I'm not. I have a lot of work I need to catch up on, being away at court so much the last few weeks."

"I am and I'd be glad to help." Art spoke up, his eyes watching the couple in front of him.

"That would be good. Listen, I think you need to take this paperwork. It's seems to be part of your investigation." Ciaran reached to stack the papers as MaKenna went to find a large envelope in his office.

"I'm sure it is. Thanks, Ciaran. You've just increased the workload, you know."

Ciaran laughed. "Anything to help out a friend. Take care. I'll call you tomorrow with the address and time."

Ciaran watched the two men pull away from where he stood in the front yard, then lifted his eyes to stare around. Emma moved around him on her leash, sniffing the night air. A low growl came from her, and Ciaran turned in the direction she was looking, not seeing anything but knowing Emma had sensed something.

"Come on, Lady Em. Let's go find our Lady MaKenna and close up the house for the night. I know you sense something there but we're not running around at night, chasing shadows."

The man standing under the tree at the edge of the yard watched as man and dog disappeared into the house. He cursed, knowing they were getting close to what he wanted to find. Somehow, he had to outsmart them and find it first. Or if they found it, get it from them. What Timothy Wilson had hidden away and threatened him with would put him in prison for the rest of his life and that he would never allow. It would also put his wife and son away. He turned and walked away, his eyes searching for law enforcement personnel.

Saturday morning came and Ciaran waited at the door for MaKenna to come towards him. She was delaying it, he knew, and he sighed. It was going to be a hard day for her. Riordan had called late last night and was meeting them at the storage unit. He hadn't told MaKenna yet. He planned to when they were on their way.

"Ready, love?" He reached for her hand, feeling the chill in her fingers. "Are you sure you want to do this? I can do it for you. You don't have to come."

She shook her head even as she headed for the door, loosening her hand from his. "I have to, Ciaran. Everything so far has been directed at me. I want to know why and who. If this solves that, then that's the way it will be."

He nodded, shutting and locking the door, and then helping her into his truck. He rounded the front, a frown on his face. Someone was out there again, he was sure. He wished whoever it was would come out into the open.

"Riordan's meeting us, isn't he?" MaKenna's voice was quiet.

"He is. He called me last night while you were outside with Emma. I wasn't keeping it from you."

"I know you weren't. I thought he'd be here." She paused. "Ciaran, will you pray about this when we get there? I know we prayed this morning, but we need to bathe this in prayer. This is going to be the turning point, I just know it."

He nodded. "I can do that." He pulled to a stop and then backed up in front of the unit. "We can load anything onto the truck that we want to take with us. Did your Mom say if the boxes were marked in any way?"

"She wrote his name all over them, she said. She did that so Dad couldn't throw anything away."

Riordan was waiting for them and took the key MaKenna handed him, studying his sister as he did so. She had a look about her he had never seen before.

"Are you ready, MaKenna?" At her nod, he unlocked the unit, pocketing the key and rolling up the door.

MaKenna wrapped her arms around herself as she stood, staring into the unit that contained what remained of her mother's married life. "She didn't keep much, did she?"

"No, she said she only wanted what we had given her or she had brought with her. Other than Uncle Timothy's stuff."

"She said it would be all along the right side of the unit. She separated it as she stored it inside, thinking we would want to go through it at some point."

Ciaran stared at the dozen or so boxes that sat there. "Where do you want to start?"

"How be we each take a box and go through it? If we need to take the box home, then we can set it on the truck as we make that decision." MaKenna hesitated for a moment, then moved forward, her hands hesitating as she reached for the first box. Riordan followed her after a few minutes, his hands reaching for the next box.

An hour later, MaKenna sat back. "I don't see anything here that would fit the key, do you?" Both men replied in the negative as they stacked the boxes back neatly against the wall.

"I think we should go through Mom's boxes, MaKenna. Did she say we could?"

MaKenna nodded, even as she chewed on her bottom lip. "What happens if we don't find anything? Does this just die and not get followed through?"

Ciaran wrapped her in a hug, then brushed at the tears on her face. "We won't let it. We'll research and find out more about that key and what it would open. But first, let's sort through your Mom's boxes. She doesn't have that many."

Riordan watched his sister, then sighing turned to the boxes. He wished he had someone in his life to share this with. Going home to an empty house every night wasn't all that it was cracked up to be.

"MaKenna, do you have that key?" Ciaran spoke thirty minutes later as he searched through one of the last boxes. He stared down into the box.

"I do. Did you find something?" She stared at the small metal box that he lifted up.

"I remember Mom holding that at times but she never opened it."

"I don't think she could. She not like had a key. But if it wasn't Uncle Timothy's, then why did she have it?" Riordan looked around, suddenly feeling exposed. "Can we tidy up here and head back to your house before we open this?"

Ciaran shot him a look, then stared at the open unit door. "I think that's likely a good move. Is there anything you want to take from here, MaKenna?"

She shook her head even as she moved towards the truck. "Let's just leave, shall we?"

Back at their house, Ciaran set the box down on the towel MaKenna had spread out on the table. He inserted the key, hesitating to turn it. When the lock clicked, he drew a deep breath and said a prayer. This was likely the one piece of evidence they had been looking for. He raised the lid, finding documents and a journal inside.

Riordan reached for the documents as MaKenna reached for the journal. She leafed through it, her face growing sadder as she read some entries.

Riordan shared a look with her before looking back at the documents. "Ciaran, can you call Art? He needs to have these."

"MaKenna?" Ciaran's voice cut through the darkness she was feeling.

She nodded. "This journal is a confession of sorts by Uncle Timothy. He had been involved in both the counterfeiting and the drug trade but was trying to get out. Mom was after him to." She drew in a breath and with a half-sob, continued. "Dad was part of it, if not one of the top people. Riordan, he lied to us all our lives."

Riordan moved towards his sister, throwing his arms around her as she sobbed. Ciaran took a look at the siblings, knowing the grief they shared would need to be worked through.

"Art? We found the box. We need you to pick it up if you can."

"I'm in your neighbourhood now. I was heading to your place to see what you had found out. Not good, I take it?"

"No, it's not. It will help close part of the investigation, I think, from the past, but it won't close what happened to MaKenna. That may come out of your investigation into this."

Art stood, looking through the journal, then reaching for the papers. He sorted through them, his thoughts racing. This was a lot deeper than he thought, involving more high-profile people in town than he expected.

"Okay, so now, this is interesting. I'll take this all in today and leave it with the team. What more can I do for you two, sorry, three?"

"Just find them, Art. I still have someone stalking around here and hiding out. I want this over with."

MaKenna's eyes shot to her husband as he spoke. Lord, please, not that. I'm so done with this. Please, please, end this soon.

Art nodded. "That's the word we've had. That they think you have documents they want." He paced for a moment. "Here's what I'll do. I'll let the press know that you have turned over all documents you've found to the police and that you are not part of the investigation. That should help."

The man swore once again and heaved his glass of liquor at the motel wall, not caring that the glass shattered and the liquor traced a dirty brown line to the floor. His hands clenched as he listened to the reporter. Now what? He cursed again as he spun, looking for something else to throw. They had turned everything over to the police, had they? He stormed from the room and headed for Ciaran's, standing near their windows in the dark of night, listening to the quiet conversation that floated out to him through the open window. He had to change his plans, now, just because of them. He was adamant he would not go to prison.

He spun and stared at the truck, then moved quietly towards it. They would pay. He had heard them talking about going away for the day, heading somewhere to spend time away from town. He'd see how far they would get. There were lots of roads with drop-offs and twists and turns that would work to his advantage.

Ciaran shut the door behind MaKenna the next morning and walked around to slid behind the wheel of her car. They had decided to run away for the day, with a picnic lunch packed and in the trunk. Emma was left at home and was pouting, Ciaran thought, even as he grinned. She was a character, he thought, never having expected to enjoy having a dog around as much as he did her.

"All set, love?" At MaKenna's nod, he pulled from the driveway, heading to a favourite area of his on the Lake Erie.

MaKenna sat back on the blanket later that day, leaning back on her hands. "This is so peaceful and relaxing, Ciaran. Why haven't we don't this before?"

"There's been so much going on and then with you kidnapped and having to recover, we just haven't had an opportunity to do this. Once it cools off, we can bring Emma and she can play in the waves."

"She'll like that, wave herding is just her style."

"Wave herding?"

MaKenna laughed. "She's a herding dog. She'll herd them. What do you think she's been doing when she follows you all over?"

Ciaran laughed at the memory. "I didn't realize that's what she was doing. Tell me, when God blesses us with a family, will she do the same?"

MaKenna blushed at his words and then nodded. "They were originally bred to watch children in a farmyard as one of their duties. She's quite good at that."

"That she is. Now, MaKenna, have you thought about what you want to do? I'm not adverse to you helping me on the jobsite, but it can be rough at times. Some of the trades are not as clean spoken as I'd like to have you around."

She shook her head. "If we could manage with me not working, I'd like to do volunteer work for a while, until I decide. When I took my college course, I thought that would be all I ever did. I had no plans to marry, consider a family." She turned her head to find him watching her. "We need to get through what we're facing first. Have you heard from Art?"

"Not yet. He's got a lot of material to work through." He reached for her hand. "Come on, love. It's time for one more walk along the sand and then head for home. Thank you for today."

She reached up to kiss his cheek. "I'm the one who should be thanking you. You've given me a day that I needed so much."

Hand in hand they wandered along the edge of the water, content to walk without speaking. The man stood and watched, cursing them that they hadn't taken Ciaran's

truck. He shook in anger as he turned back to
his own vehicle.

Chapter 16

    *E*arly the next morning, Ciaran headed out of town, searching for the address where he had been asked to give an estimate for a kitchen renovation. Once done, he stood for a moment, taking in the trees and view from the hill. He headed for his truck, his mind on the work involved here and then shifting to the renovation he was finishing up. He sighed. If things continued the way it was, he would need to hire another carpenter to work with him.

    He hit the brakes as he neared a curve. They sank to the floor, not slowing his truck at all. He pumped at them with no effect. He reached for the gearstick, shifting down without much slowing of his vehicle. He fought to control it, his heart in his mouth as the tires whined and the truck weaved between lanes. Lord, let there be nothing coming. A sudden shift in the pavement and Ciaran knew he was fighting a losing battle. He shoved the transmission into neutral and braced himself for the impact, his truck hitting the ditch, and rolling over and over. His body was flung around inside as much as the tight seatbelt would allow. Smoke rose from the deployed airbags even as the sound of breaking glass and crunching metal filled the air. The truck landed on its tires, in view of the infrequently traveled road.

An hour later, the homeowner Ciaran had spent a couple of hours with headed down the road, a frown on his face as he followed the weaving tire marks. He slammed on his brakes and pulled to the side of the road, his phone in his hand as he ran from his truck towards Ciaran's. He yanked at the door but couldn't budge it. He carefully scraped the broken window out of his way and reached in, feeling for a pulse. Relief coursed through him as he realized Ciaran was alive.

The firefighters and paramedics worked to free Ciaran as the homeowner spoke with the responding patrol officer. When he gave Ciaran's name, the officer's head came up and he held up a hand for the man.

"Just a moment. I need to call another officer." He reached for his radio, asking his dispatch to contact Art. "Sorry about that. Now continue."

The two men turned as they heard the sound of the breaking glass from the windshield and then the sound of the equipment in use to pull the dashboard away from Ciaran's body. The tarp used to cover him while the windshield was removed and he was quickly pulled from the vehicle. Stabilizing him with a neck brace and then onto a Stryker backboard, he was wheeled quickly to the waiting ambulance and sirens sounded as it left, rushing him to the hospital in his hometown.

✮ ✮ ✮ ✮ ✮

An hour later, Angus stood at his son's bedside, allowed in briefly by the Emergency Room staff. Art found him there, a question on his face.

"How is he, Angus?" 

Angus shrugged. "We're still waiting on tests and that kind of stuff. What happened, Art?"

"I'm still piecing it together. But where is MaKenna?"

Angus looked around, his mind coming out of the fog it had gone into when he got the call. "She's not here? She should be." Then he groaned. "They called me. He

254

hasn't changed his contact information." He reached for his keys.

"Let me. I'll have a patrol officer go by and bring her in."

Angus nodded. "Thanks, Art."

"And Angus? There will be a patrol officer outside here that goes with him wherever he goes."

Angus stopped, his eyes on Art. "This wasn't an accident?"

"Not from what the resounding patrol officer has indicated. His brakes weren't working. I'm having his truck towed to our garage. We'll know more in a couple of days."

★ ★ ★ ★ ★

MaKenna worked away in her kitchen, her eyes on the food she was preparing for a friend who was sick. She heard the doorbell and grabbing a towel, wiped at her hands. She peeked out, not seeing anyone, and moved to another window to get a better look at the driveway. Not a vehicle there, other than hers. She shrugged. I guess they had the wrong house, she thought, as she headed back towards the kitchen, stopping to pet Emma as she made her way by her. She knew Ciaran

255

would be late getting home that night, he had already warned her.

She washed up again, and then, her back to the door, continued working. A low growl from Emma brought her head up just as she heard the snick of the closing door. She froze, then tried to turn, but a heavy hand had grasped her hair, pulling her head back and preventing her from moving. A knife appeared in her sight and she started to shake.

"It's taken a while to finally get you alone, but now you are. No one's coming to your rescue."

Emma stood and growled at the man holding MaKenna. The man's hand pulled her head back further and she cried out with the pain.

"Put your dog away or she's dead."

MaKenna was shoved towards Emma, just catching her balance. She reached for Emma, who tried to move past her.

"Come on, Emma. In your crate, girl. Please, Emma. Now." Fastening the crate was one of the hardest things she had done. Emma fought to get back out, to protect her mistress, the growls and barks sounding loud in the house.

The man had followed her and grabbed at her hair again, using that restriction to move her back into the kitchen. She fought him until she felt the knife against her ribs.

"No fighting, my dear. We're going somewhere we can have a long talk. No one's coming to your rescue, least of all your husband." His breath hit her ear and she shrank back from him.

A ring at the doorbell stopped his words, and he turned that way, dragging her with him.

"Get rid of whoever that is. Now!"

MaKenna nodded her head, feeling his hand leave her hair and shove her towards the door. She hesitated to catch her breath, before she opened in, her eyes staring at the young patrol officer standing there.

"Can I help you?" She had to work to get the words out in a normal manner, knowing her assailant was standing behind the open door.

"Mrs. Quinn? I was asked to come and give you a ride to the hospital. Your husband was in a motor vehicle accident earlier."

"Ciaran?" Shock paled her face even more that it was. "No! Not Ciaran!"

Without thinking, she stepped towards the door, and then felt herself yanked backwards.

The patrol officer's hand went to his weapon even as he moved towards her, his eyes locked on the door.

"No! Don't come in! He has a knife!" MaKenna threw herself towards him, to prevent him from coming in.

Her assailant shot from behind the door, shoving her aside and attacking the young officer, leaving him bleeding on the doorstep, the door wide open. He turned to find her, running after her and tackling her to the ground. She struggled to get away, but his weight kept her pinned to the ground. She was yanked to her feet, her hands bound in front of her, and then shoved towards the backyard and through the gate, and finally shoved violently into the backseat of a waiting car, her assailant climbing in beside her, the knife once more to her ribs. Tears streamed down her face, as her thoughts went to Ciaran. Lord, please let him be alive. Take me, but let him live.

Art paced restlessly outside Ciaran's room where the evaluation was still ongoing. MaKenna should have been here by now, he knew. He reached for his phone, asking their dispatch to do a welfare check on their address. Angus paused in the doorway as he left Ciaran's room, his eyes on the younger man.

"Where's MaKenna?"

"I know. She should have been here by now and isn't. I've just asked someone to go find out what's wrong." He nodded his chin towards Ciaran. He could see they had taken off the cervical collar and seemed to be getting ready to move him.

"They're sending him up to the floor, they said. Nothing broken, thank God. Lots of bruises. A concussion. Sprained wrist. Cuts from the broken glass. He has a large cut on his thigh as well, from what they couldn't or wouldn't tell me. He's alive, but battered."

Art nodded, his eyes going to his phone as it chimed, and he answered it. Angus watched his eyes slide closed even as he turned back to Ciaran, hearing his son speak.

"Ciaran? How are you feeling?" Angus stood at the bedside, his eyes assessing his son.

"Like I was run over by a Mack truck. What happened?"

"You were in an accident coming back from doing an estimate as best we can figure out. Do you remember anything?"

Ciaran shook his head, but regretted doing that as the pain sliced through it. "No, not really. I think my brakes failed, and they shouldn't have." He lifted his head slightly and looked around. "Where's MaKenna?"

"We have someone bringing her in. Did you know you haven't changed your next of kin here yet? I got the call instead of MaKenna."

He groaned. "I haven't been here since we married for myself, just MaKenna. Wake me when she gets her." His eyes closed and he slept, his sleep deep.

Art stopped beside Angus. "How is he?"

"He doesn't remember much, other than his brakes failed. He's hurting, Art." He turned to watch his friend's face, not liking the grimness there. "Where's MaKenna?"

"I don't know. Another patrol officer responded,   found   the   first   officer unconscious on the floor, Emma in her crate, and MaKenna gone. He said the grass was disturbed on the front ground like there had been a struggle. He followed footsteps to the back gate. He thinks she was taken out through there to a car. He saw evidence of a waiting vehicle."

Angus' eyes slid shut as he groaned. "Not again, please, Lord. We need MaKenna here with Ciaran. He eyed the detective. "Now what?"

"Now we search. I have an idea of where she may be and I'm heading that way. Keep me posted on Ciaran."

Angus watched as the detective strode away, determination in every step. He would bring MaKenna back as soon as he could. Angus sighed, then stepped aside as the nurses came to move Ciaran to the floor. Lord, I have no idea what's going on right now, but You are in control. Protect my son's lady.

MaKenna felt herself dragged from the vehicle and shoved into a house, down a hallway and then into a room. She refused to raise her eyes even as she was pushed down into a chair. She winced as her elbow hit the wooden back of the chair. Her chin was grabbed roughly and her face raised. She stared at the man in front of her, realizing he was the man who had accosted her about the box, and then had stood watching her all those weeks ago.

"Not so cocky now, are we, lady?" He gave a laugh, and then moved back to lean against the desk, his feet crossed at the ankles. He slid the knife he had been holding onto the desk and laughed coarsely as she cringed at the sight.

"You're staying here, lady. For now anyway. There's someone who wants to talk to you. He'll be in shortly. Don't bother trying to escape. You won't get far. We have guard dogs outside and the windows are alarmed and the alarm set."

He laughed again as he stood and moved away to the door, picking up the knife again as he did so.

MaKenna heard the snick of the lock and then slumped into the chair, her eyes searching for a way out. She worked at the knot on her bonds, her teeth tearing at the rope, finally working the knot enough she could slide her wrists free. She shook off the rope and stood, searching the room.

She heard the door open behind her and stood still, her back to it, not turning around as she heard footsteps behind her. She felt the man standing, staring at her, felt the anger emanating from him.

"Well, Dad? What's this about?"

She finally turned, her eyes on her father, waiting for him to speak.

Her father stood, his eyes filled with anger and loathing, hatred covering his face.

"You just couldn't let it lie, could you, girl? You had to keep digging. You just had to buy that house, didn't you?" His body shook, the rage was so great.

"Didn't plan on that happening, you know. I had no idea you had a connection to that house. When did you kill Uncle Timothy anyway? And why?"

She stared at him from the floor, her hand on her face where he had struck her, blood dripping from the cut on her lip. "Sure, go ahead. Slap me around. You always wanted to, didn't you?" She was baiting him, trying to get answers to questions that had plagued her the whole of her life. "I'm glad Mom and Riordan are away from you."

"Not for long. Once I'm finished with you, I'll go get my wife. She's not allowed to be where she is. She's only allowed at my side."

MaKenna rose to her feet, seeing fully for the first time the rage in her father. She knew he had been like that at times but now he was out of control. She feared for her life, but she feared even more for her mother. *Keep them safe, dear Lord. Don't let him hurt them again.*

"You weren't supposed to get away. You weren't to go to school and then move away. You were to stay in my home all your life." Spittle flew from his mouth as he paced the floor in front of her.

"Didn't happen, did it? I couldn't stay. There is no way I would have." She backed up, hitting the shelf behind her as he approached her again, hand raised to strike her again. "Go ahead. Hit me all you want. It won't solve anything."

He stared at her before lowering his hand. "No, it won't. But I took care of your husband. He's dead."

She shook her head. "No, he's not. And if you try to get to him now, you or your men or whoever it is that's in your pocket, won't reach him. He'll be under police protection."

She taunted him, knowing full well that he was almost all the way over the edge of sanity. If she could keep him talking, maybe someone would find her.

He raised his hand again and this time she couldn't duck. He stared at her crumpled body and then at his hand, turning and walking away. He would be back and she would tell him exactly what he wanted to know. She had to know where the money and jewels he had stolen were hidden. She just had to. His man had watched them search, finding keys to boxes. He knew Timothy had hidden that package well, just not where.

He turned once more at the doorway, his eyes on the woman he had called daughter. The brother and sister had never known he wasn't their biological father, that he had married their mother when MaKenna was four. Riordan had been made to forget that he had had another father. Conditioning over the years had driven that deep within him, and the man knew it would take a lot to bring it back to him. He slammed his hand on the door, relishing the hurt. He needed that box, that money and jewels. He had debts that he had to pay and those men wouldn't be put off much longer.

Ciaran stirred, his headache better. His body protested the moves, but he sat up, his eyes searching the room and not finding MaKenna. Riordan slumped in the chair beside him, his eyes closed as he slept. Ciaran reached for the bedrail, lowering it and sliding to the edge of the bed, waiting for the dizziness to dissipate before he stood on wobbly feet. He searched the room, finding his clothes.

"Where are you going, Ciaran?" Riordan's sleep-roughened voice startled him.

"I'm leaving. I need to find MaKenna."

"Did I miss something and you've been discharged?" Riordan stood and stretched, his hands reaching for the ceiling, before he lowered them and tucked his shirt back into his jeans.

"No, I haven't been. But I need to search for her." He moved and waited for the headache to ease. "I can't lie in here while she's missing."

"They are looking for her, you know."

"I know, but I need to search." He eyed Riordan. "Did your uncle own any property that you know of?"

Riordan shook his head. "No, not that I know of. Why?"

"Because I think your father is the one who took her and is holding her somewhere until he can find whatever it is he's been after."

"That makes sense." Riordan shot a look at the door. "It's not going to be easy to get you out of here. There's an officer at the door and one at the elevator."

Ciaran grinned. "The stairs. They won't be looking for us there. Can you distract the officer at the door for a moment until I reach the stairway? I'll meet you at the back of the building."

Riordan hesitated, his eyes on Ciaran, before he nodded. "I think we need to go talk to Mom. I'm remembering things from when I was young, and somehow I don't think the man I call Dad is actually my father."

"What?" Ciaran paused as he pulled on his jacket. "Are you serious? You're just remembering it now?" He looked down at his jeans, muttering to himself about needing fresh clothing.

Riordan nodded. "I am. I don't know why I couldn't before. I felt something niggling at me all along. This must be it. I know I was young when he came into our lives. I don't think MaKenna remembers that."

"Okay, let's put our plan into action. It's still early right?"

"Yeah, it is. About three o'clock. Not much action going on here. Are you sure you're well enough?"

"Doesn't matter. I'm leaving." With that said, he pointed at the door.

Fifteen minutes later, the nurse stood in the door, her mouth dropping open and she turned to speak to the officer, who shot her a look and then stared into the room as well. He groaned. So much for watching his charge! He just hoped he wasn't demoted or something because of it.

Riordan pulled up to his mother's home, looking across the seat at Ciaran.

"Are you still sure you need to do this? It means waking Mom up."

"We have to, Ciaran. And I'll wager that your Mom's not sleeping. I can see light around the curtain."

Sarah stood at the open door, watching the two men walk towards her. She pointed to the kitchen.

"Come, sit. I have coffee or tea, whichever you prefer."

"Thanks, Sarah." Ciaran sank in the chair, grateful to be off his feet. He wasn't feeling as well as he tried to let on.

"Mom, we need to talk." Riordan rolled the mug around in his hands. "I've been remembering some things." His eyes raised, regret in them, as he continued. "Dad isn't my real father, is he?"

She shook her head, tears flowing down her face. "No, he's not, and I am so thankful that he isn't. I don't know what I was thinking when I married him, but he wasn't like this before. He changed after your uncle died."

"Do you think he had a hand in that?"

She nodded. "I have had that suspicion all these years. I searched his belongings, his papers, but found nothing to prove it or even hint at it. I always felt he was involved in crime somehow, that his job as an insurance agent really was just a front."

"Wait a moment. He's an insurance agent?" Ciaran raised a hand to stop her. "What kind of insurance?"

She stared at him. "House insurance. Contents insurance. Not life insurance."

Ciaran's eyes slid shut. "That's what we've been looking for all along. Theft and cover up. Insurance fraud."

"What are you talking about?" Riordan spun to stare at him.

"He gets people to insure their belongings, particularly jewelry or valuable antiques or paintings. Then he has them stolen and sold on the black market."

Riordan's eyes met his mother's and he saw the dawning comprehension in hers. "That's how he had so much money at times. Ciaran, did your father ever finish his investigation into the financials?"

"I'm not sure that he has. He's been pulled in so many directions lately with his investigations. I'll call him in the morning and ask. But right now, we need to think of where he might be holding her." He turned to Sarah. "Did your brother have a home somewhere? How about your first husband?"

She went to shake her head, then paused. "Timothy never did. He had too much wanderlust in his soul. But Samuel? He did. I thought it was sold, but maybe it wasn't. I thought Darby said it had been."

"What's the address? And do you have a computer?" Ciaran was on his feet.

"Maybe I can do a search and see if it's still registered to him."

"How, Ciaran? You don't have access to that kind of information."

"But I may be able to access voter registration lists from then. If not, I'll call Art." He groaned as he gripped the chair in front of him. "Art! How do I face him now?"

Riordan started to laugh, drawing a black look from Ciaran. "You should have thought of that before you did a disappearing act. I hope you let him know you tricked the officer outside your door."

"That wasn't me." Ciaran smirked. "That was you."

"But it was your plan."

Sarah stared between the two. "Are you telling me you weren't discharged, Ciaran?"

"That's what he's saying, Mom. He went AWOL."

"I think the correct term is left against medical advice. However, let's get on with what we need to do."

Sarah rose and pointed the way to the computer. "While you two are searching, I'll make you breakfast. At least then, I'll know you've had something to eat and are ready to face the day. And I have some clean clothes that you can borrow. I don't think you're going to want to be wandering around in tattered clothing." She paused as Riordan's phone chimed.

He pulled it out, read the text, and grinned at Ciaran. "You've been found out. Art's looking for you."

Chapter 17

Ciaran sat back from the computer, his hand reaching for the cup of coffee. He sipped, grimacing at the taste of cold coffee. He set the cup back down, his eyes on the screen as he scrolled through the voter's list. He sighed. This was not finding what he needed to find. He rose, stretched and then limped over the counter, dumping out the coffee in his cup and refilling it. Riordan and his mother were in the living room, their conversation quiet. He really wanted this to end but he knew he had to find that house.

He turned as he heard a knock at the door and saw Riordan heading for the door. It was still early morning, but he figured someone had tracked him down. He watched at his father entered, followed by Art. He sighed. Now, to face the two he had been trying to avoid.

"Ciaran?" His father walked towards him. "Here, your mom sent you some clean clothes."

"Thanks, Dad." He kept his head down, not quite sure how to approach his father.

"Checked yourself out, did you?" His father's voice held a trace of humour. "Can't say as I blame you. I would probably have done the same." His hand rested on his son's shoulder. "Look at me, Ciaran." Ciaran stared into the eyes so much like his. "I know you're worried, son, but you have to stay healthy yourself."

Ciaran nodded. "I know, Dad, but I couldn't just lay there. I had to do something."

Art spoke. "The officer's a little worried, you know. He was afraid he'd be reprimanded. Between the two of you, you certainly caused a stir there. Luckily one of the nurses saw Ciaran disappearing through the door."

Ciaran sighed. "Where do we stand, Art? Have you found her?"

Art shook his head. "Not yet, but we're working hard to find her. Looks as if you have been too."

Ciaran nodded. "We have been. Sarah mentioned that her husband was involved in the insurance business."

"I am aware of that. What of it?" Art waited to hear where Ciaran was going with that.

"Say he has home owners purchase insurance. Then, he steals whatever and sells it on the black market. I would say likely that the homeowners are innocent victims. He could pick and choose who he wanted to steal from."

"Now, that's an idea that we didn't give much credence to. Why do you think that?"

Riordan spoke up. "It makes sense, Art. He would have money, lots of it at times, and that he would have after he had been away or had traveled somewhere."

Art stared between the two men and then sighed. "Are you sure you're not detectives?" He reached for his phone. "Let me call one of my team and get them started looking at that."

"Art, wait. Before you call, there's something else we need to discuss with you." Ciaran shared a look with Riordan, who sighed and then nodded. "The man you are looking for? He's Sarah's second husband. We're trying to track down a home that her first husband, Samuel, owned. She thought it was sold, but now she's not sure. If it isn't, could he have MaKenna there?"

Art's hand stilled, his eyes on Ciaran. "That is a possibility. Let me see what my team can come up with." He finally pocketed his phone. "It will take a bit, but Sue's good at finding these places. I don't know how she does it. Now, where were you two at?"

"Nowhere." Ciaran sounded disgruntled. "I just want my wife back."

"We know you do, son. Look, go and get cleaned up and let me have the clothes you're wearing. Sarah's offered to make us some breakfast and I think that's a good idea."

Ciaran stared at his father for a moment, then nodded before he turned and walked away. His father's body sagged as he watched his son walk away. He felt Riordan's hand on his shoulder, but the comfort of a friend didn't help. He wanted to make it all better for him and couldn't. Lord, now what? Where do we turn to now? Lead our steps, dear Lord, and keep our precious MaKenna safe.

Art pulled out his phone, frowning as he read the text. "They pulled fingerprints from your house, Ciaran. They belong to a Robert Nelson. Do you know him?"

Ciaran shook his head as he towelled his hair dry. "No, I don't. Do you have a photo?"

Art held up his phone. "Do you recognize him?"

"I do. He's the one we've been telling you about. He's the one who took MaKenna?"

"It appears that way. Now, what?" Art grumbled as he pulled his phone back and answered it, moving outside to talk.

Ciaran watched him walk away before he spoke. "I don't think he's getting too far, do you? Dad, did you ever finish the financials you were looking Ito?"

"I did. Darby has large deposits of money every month or two, and there is no way he'd make that with insurance sales."

Sarah nodded. "I saw those when I was looking through his paperwork. I never once thought he was a thief." She turned to Riordan. "Oh, son, what have I done?"

"You didn't do anything, Mom. It's Darby. I just wish I knew where MaKenna is."

MaKenna pulled herself up to sitting position from the floor, her back to the bookshelf as she rubbed at her face. She would have a nice-sized bruise there, she thought. Through blurry eyes, she stared around, trying to understand what had happened. She crawled to her feet, holding on to the bookshelf until her head cleared. It was dark, with just a crack of dawn peeking through on the horizon. She stumbled to the window and hands on the panes of glass, stared out. She frowned, thinking back to what she had been told. Where were the dogs? Had that all been a lie? She reached for the lock on the door and flicked it off, pushing open the door. No alarm, she thought. Now, can I get away or has this been a set-up to trap her? She shot a look back at the room door, then stepped through the door into the outdoors. She shivered in the cool air and then trudged across the lawn, her feet sinking into the grass. It had been warm enough overnight that no dew had formed.

She stared around, trying to get her bearings, and then headed for the trees she could see in the distance. She prayed that she would make it before anyone knew she was gone. She hadn't heard anyone come near her, and she had been awake for most of the night, laying still to fool anyone who stood over her.

Reaching the trees, she looked back. It had taken her longer to get there than she thought it would. She sighed, her throat and mouth dry, but she knew she had to continue on. She set her face towards the rising sun, not sure where she was going or if she would even make it.

She didn't hear the roar of anger from behind her or the smashing of glass. Her stepfather had found her missing and someone's head would roll, he declared. He stormed to the open door and stepped out into the yard. He could see no trace of where she had gone. He stormed back in, shouting orders, causing the men with him to run to do his bidding.

He threw the door open as the doorbell rang, staring at the men standing there.

"What do you want? Get out of here!" He started to slam the door until the man standing there spoke.

"Darby Dunne, you're under arrest for murder, attempted murder, assault, fraud, theft. That's just for starters." Art motioned to one of the uniformed officers who moved forward, handcuffs in hand.

"I don't think so." He flicked his glance over the men standing there, his eyes stopping on Ciaran. "What's he doing here? Have him arrested for trespassing."

Art turned to stare at Ciaran. "Really? Trespass? Oh, I forgot. I need to add that to the list of charges you're facing. This house doesn't belong to you. It belonged to Sarah's first husband, Samuel Andrews, who willed it to his wife. So you see, you're the trespasser. I understand from Sarah that she had no idea you were using it and that she had never given permission for you to do just that."

Art pushed past Darby, Ciaran and Riordan on his heels, followed by a number of officers. "Where is she, Darby?"

"Who? There's no female here."

"Ah, but there was." Art spun to stare at him, his hand stopping Ciaran from moving towards him. "We have evidence and eye witness accounts that MaKenna was here and that she was subjected to an assault at your hands. Now, where is she?" The officers who had searched the house returned, shaking their heads.

Darby began to laugh, a laugh filled with pure evil. "She's gone and you'll never find her."

Riordan's arms came around Ciaran to hold him away from the man. Ciaran struggled to get away, wanting to take on the man.

"Riordan, take Ciaran outside. We'll search here again."

Riordan kept his arms around Ciaran until he wrestled him from the house, Ciaran shaking himself loose as he walked away from the house.

"Where is she, Riordan? She was here." Ciaran's voice broke as he struggled with his emotions, his eyes searching for her.

"I know, Ciaran. Where would she go?" He paced the lawn, finally heading around the back, his eyes on the house and then the trees.

"Riordan, didn't Art say she had been held in a room at the back of the house?" Ciaran turned in a circle, his hand going to the wound on his thigh. "What if she came out the back door, that one there?" He pointed at the door leading to the office. "Where would she head?"

"Not around front. She'd be afraid she'd be captured again." Riordan spun in a circle as well, trying to think like his sister. "There. That way, Ciaran. She'd head for the trees and hope for cover. But how long a start has she had?"

Ciaran nodded, his eyes tracing the woods. "A straight line to start with, to get out of sight as soon as she could. She'd be heading east, wouldn't she?"

"That she would. Stay here. I'll see if I can find some water and what not to take with us. Are you sure you're up to a hike?"

Ciaran nodded. "It doesn't matter about me. I need to find MaKenna."

Art spoke from beside him. "Let me send some officers with you. That way, you'll have support if you need it." He studied his friend. "I don't know if you're able to do this, Ciaran."

Ciaran shrugged off the concern, heading for the trees. "I just want my wife home, Art. That's all that matters."

Art watched as Ciaran limped away, his concern that Ciaran would not make it very far or would end up hurt worse than he already was.

✫ ✫ ✫ ✫ ✫

MaKenna searched the woods, her head hurting and her eyes blurring. She was tired, hurting from the beating she had taken, thirsty, and just wanting to go home. She had no idea where she was. She turned in a circle, fighting the dizziness she was feeling. Why, Lord, she thought? Why did this have to happen?

She turned again, then stopped, her eyes finding a building in front of her, not close, she knew. She walked towards it, the thought going through her mind that God had provided a strong tower for her to run to. Lord, let them find me please. I can't go on much further.

She fumbled with the door, finding the latch and shoving the door open. The room was round, dusty and littered with debris. She didn't care. She dropped to her knees, her hands hitting the floor as well. She finally gave into the fatigue and pain she had been fighting and let her body collapse, her head nestling on one arm.

Ciaran reached for the door a couple of hours later, a frown in place that the door was open. He shared a look with Riordan and then with the two officers with them. The officers had wanted to head in another direction, but Ciaran had been adamant they were searching in the right direction. He pushed at the door, his eyes staring into the dimness. He heard Riordan's low cry and turned. Riordan was pointing the floor and he followed the line of his finger.

"MaKenna!" The cry was wrenched from his body as he threw himself to his knees beside her, reaching to scoop her into his arms, cuddling her close. Riordan crouched beside him, his hand reaching to touch his sister.

The two officers shared a look and then one pulled out his radio, giving their location, and asking for a chopper to fly in. There was no way those two would be able to walk out.

An hour later, Ciaran sat beside his wife's hospital bed, watching as the medical team worked around her.

"Ciaran?" He looked up as Dan spoke to him. "She'll be okay. She's dehydrated, has some bruising on her face, but overall, she's in good shape. Now, about you. How's the leg?"

"The leg? Oh, that leg. It's sore. I didn't break open any of the stitches."

Dan nodded, knowing that was all he would get from his friend. "Watch it closely, okay? I don't want you back in here with an infection."

Ciaran vaguely nodded as his eyes went back to MaKenna. He reached to clasp her hand in his. He nodded as the nurses spoke to him, just wanting her to wake up.

MaKenna stirred, her head clearer than it had been. She frowned before her eyes fully opened. Why was the floor of the building so soft and where did the blankets come from? And who was holding her hand so tight? She tugged to release it but whoever was holding it just tightened the grip.

Her eyes searched the room. A hospital room, she thought. Now the soft bed and blankets made sense, but not the grip on her hand. Her head turned slightly and she frowned again, blinking at the man standing there.

"MaKenna? Can you hear me?" Ciaran's voice was soft.

She nodded, swallowing hard against the dryness in her throat. Ciaran's hand moved to raise her head as he held a glass to her mouth and helped her drink. Setting the glass back down, he laid his hand on her cheek.

"Welcome home, love. I missed you."

"How long, Ciaran?"

"Thirty-six hours or so. You're safe, love. Art's arrested everyone involved. He's sorting through it all. He'll want to talk to you later and get a statement from you. But you're home."

Tears sparkled in her eyes and trickled down her cheeks. "You're okay, Ciaran? I worried about you. The officer who came to the door said you had been in an accident."

"Some bumps and bruises, cuts. But I'll get there." He sat, his chin on his hands grasping the bedrail. "We need to stop doing this, you know?"

"Doing what?"

"Meeting in a hospital room. It's getting old." He gave her a cheeky grin.

She smiled even as she shook her head. "That we do. When can I go home?"

"The nurses said if you were awake and able to get around, once the IV finished then you'd be able to leave. Emma's looking for you."

"Emma? She's okay. What happened to her? I was forced to crate her and she tried so hard to get back out."

"Beth came and got her. She'll bring her home later today." Ciaran was silent for a moment. "I prayed so hard you'd find somewhere safe. And you did. That building was an old watch tower from years ago."

"It was? I guess it's still a place of refuge, then, isn't it?"

Three hours later, Ciaran carried MaKenna into their home and headed for the bedroom. She was under strict orders of bedrest for the next couple of days. She was asleep before he laid her down, pulling the blankets up to cover her. He stood for a moment, indecision in his demeanour before he pulled off his shoes and laid down beside her, cuddling her close, not wanting to let her go. He sighed. Now what, Lord? She's home but she has to heal. We still have so much stuff to sort through and I'm not sure she's up to it. He yawned, before his own eyes closed and he too slept.

Chapter 18

A week later, Ciaran sat on the couch in their living room, MaKenna tight in his arms and watched their family mingle around, all trying to find a seat. Art had asked to meet with them and bring them up to date on what was happening with the case.

MaKenna shifted in his arms, her own arms encircling Emma who lay across both their laps, occasionally swiping a tongue across MaKenna's arm or face. Riordan had settled down on the other end of the couch, his body angled so he could watch his sister.

Finally, Art cleared his throat, drawing their attention to him. He reached for the folder he had laid on the coffee table when he can come in, leaving it there while they had shared a meal and laughter.

Art searched the faces of those around him. "Ciaran, MaKenna. It's over. It's been tough for you, but it's now over.

Ciaran nodded. "Before you continue, let me guess. You've been able to tie Darby to multiple robberies over the years? In the millions, I suspect."

"That's correct, Ciaran. We're trying to track the jewels and pieces of art but we're not likely to find them."

MaKenna turned to stare at Ciaran. "Darby really was a piece of work, wasn't he? To think he tried so hard to make me a shadow of what I am, to keep me under his thumb. I wonder what he would have done if I hadn't gone to school and moved away."

"You would have had no life. If you had married, it would have been to someone just like him, I suspect. The house, Art. Was it in Darby's name or still in Timothy's?"

"Still in Timothy's, not Samuel's as we thought. He couldn't change the title without Sarah's consent and he wouldn't ask for that."

Ciaran nodded. "That's what we thought. Now, what was his whole plan? Did he come up with this on the fly or had he planned it for years?"

"He's not talking but we think he planned for years and laid out his own long-term goals. Part of that was to get his hands on the trust funds set up for Timothy's family."

MaKenna spoke up. "That's what I don't understand. Where did that money come from? If it's from crime, I want no part of it."

"It's not, Sarah. Dad looked into it. Timothy had been left some money by a cousin and he invested it. His investments paid off in huge dividends. He had no family of his own and decided to leave it to you two." Ciaran shared a look with Riordan over MaKenna's head. "It's free and clear and now in your hands. It's up to you two whether you keep it or not. There was no way that Darby could ever had gotten his hands on it, no matter what he tried.

"Dad was also able to track Darby's financials for the last twenty years or so. Don't ask how he did it. It's some magic that he knows how to work. Darby didn't make a real good living from his insurance business. In fact, in the last few years, he hasn't made any money that way. He's been living off the proceeds of his crime but he also borrowed money from a loan shark. He wanted your trust funds to pay that off."

Ciaran paused as he watched MaKenna's face. "What are you thinking?"

She shrugged. "That's what is was with him all the time. Money. Why are people like that?"

Ciaran shrugged, then continued. "Art said he traced your uncle's last few days as best he could. What we surmise happened is this and we can't confirm it at all. Your uncle seems to have stumbled onto Darby's criminal activities and threatened to expose him. He hid the keys that we found around here, not trusting that Darby wouldn't find them if he left them in his apartment. He knew Darby had searched it many times."

Riordan spoke up. "Did Uncle Timothy's journal tell you that?"

Art nodded. "It did. It held a wealth of information."

"And that's why Darby wanted to get his hands on it so badly. He wanted to destroy it after he had found the keys and any other information he had on him. The man who terrorized us and followed us has been Darby's bodyguard for years. He did a lot of the dirty work for him. Darby paid him well."

"How did you find me though?" MaKenna searched the faces of her husband and Art.

"Pure fluke or should I say, God?" Ciaran tightened his hold on her. "Art's team was able to find an address for the house and verify that the utilities were still on, paid through a numbered company. And that company led to Darby."

"Really? This just gets stranger all the time. Did they ever find out what killed Uncle Timothy?"

"Darby said they had been arguing and Timothy was going to the police. Darby shoved him and Timothy fell, striking his head. Darby thought he was dead, stabbed him to make sure and then boarded him up behind the drywall. The family didn't live in the house for a couple of years, waiting for renovations to be finished, and Darby made sure that took time. We'll never know if that was true or not."

MaKenna shuddered. "That's horrible. But then, Darby has no soul."

Sarah stared at her daughter. "That's a strange thing to say."

MaKenna shrugged. "It's the truth." She turned her head to watch Ciaran's face. "What else do we know?"

"Timothy threw a few things in to confuse Darby and consequently confused us. Two of those keys were that, the building in the woods for one. Darby is the one who had Dr. Stirling kidnapped, had you kidnapped, had Anna disappear. He was behind everything that happened. Even the woman who showed up at the door that day was hired by him. She's an actress and was told to play a part of a sister and demand to enter the house. So was the older man."

"He did all that? I still don't get it." MaKenna was confused.

"I don't think we'll totally understand everything, MaKenna. He's the one who had the counterfeiting operation going, and Dad has traced a bank account that he thinks is connected to that. Art has been able to close the portion of the tale about the drugs. Darby had been involved in that when he was a teenager and into his early twenties. He got out of that when he started stealing jewelry and art."

"And he's the one who had your truck tampered with?"

Ciaran nodded. "Art found out that there were holes punched in the brake lines, which led to a slow leak of brake fluid. He really didn't care where or when I had an accident. He told Art that he was hoping I was killed, that way you'd come back to stay with your Mom and he could gain control of your trust fund."

Angus finally spoke up. "He was truly an evil man. I don't know, Art, if you'll ever find out what all he's done."

Art nodded. "I'm sure we won't. The bodyguard has agreed to talk, for a lighter sentence. He's admitted his part in the assaults and kidnappings. He also admitted being the ones to leave the voice mail, the texts, the packages, the cards, for you, MaKenna, at your step-father's request, hoping to chase you back home."

MaKenna leaned back on Ciaran, her hands idly stroking Emma's fur. Emma shifted on her knee, seeking to get closer to her mistress. After what had happened, Emma didn't let her get far out of her sight.

"Is that it, then?" MaKenna looked around. "Do we have answers for everything?"

"I'm not sure that we do, MaKenna." Angus leaned forward, his arms on his thighs, hands clasped, his eyes studying the young couple, then turning to Riordan. "You three and Sarah as well have a lot of healing to do. We may never know what all they planned or did. I'm sure there are things that were moved or taken that they were involved in.

All I can say is that I'm glad you two are with us and in one piece."

Ciaran nodded. "Me, too, Dad. I just wish we hadn't had to go through what we did." He looked up as the doorbell rang. "Were we expecting someone else?"

"Not that I'm aware of." Angus stood and headed for the door. They could hear a quiet conversation before Angus returned, holding an envelope in his hand.

"Not another one of those. Please. Didn't Darby already do this?" MaKenna's shrank back from it.

"Actually, MaKenna, I don't think he had anything to do with this. It's from a lawyer's office."

"Great! Now he's suing us for having him arrested, for abuse of position, for damages." They laughed at her grumbling even as Ciaran reached to take the envelope from his father.

He studied it, then tilted his head to watch his wife's face. He didn't like the fear he saw there.

"We can open it or not, MaKenna. It is from a lawyer, but not from a neighbouring town. Big city stuff."

She shook her head. "I don't want to know what's in there." She went to stand, but Ciaran pulled her back down.

"MaKenna, we need to do this. We'll always wonder what it was about if we don't."

"Then let someone else open it." She grabbed it out of his hand and gave it to Riordan. "Here. You have our permission to open it."

"Are you sure, MaKenna?" Riordan passed the letter to Angus. "How be we let the senior gentleman in the room have the privilege?"

Art snickered. "This is like the old game we used to play. Hot Potato. Will someone open it already?"

His comment caused laughter to break out, much needed laughter. Emma started and then barked, jumping down to run from the room and return with her frisbee.

Angus studied the envelope one more, and then reached for his pocket knife to slit it open. He pulled out a document and read it, his eyes going to the three young people sitting on the couch. He cleared his throat, not quite sure how to continue.

"Dad?" Ciaran's voice was curious. "What is it?"

"A voice from the grave, I would say son. It's a letter from your uncle, MaKenna and Riordan. Here, Sarah. You read it."

Sarah reached for it, her hands shaking. Her brother that she thought had run away had been killed, and now she held a letter from him. She cleared her throat before she read.

Dear Children - Riordan and MaKenna

I have been so privileged to be your uncle. You have brought so much joy and happiness to my life. I can't wait to see you grow and have children of your own.

But if you're reading this, then that won't happen. My life will have been cut short.

I'm leaving a legacy for you two and your children, if God blesses you that way. It's not much, but use it the way God would have you to.

You two are a testament to the way your mom and Dad raised you. Not Darby though. Samuel and Sarah.

I love you two dearly. Enclosed in this letter is evidence that I want you to turn over to the police. It is evidence that Darby desperately wants to find, but never will. It will confirm his illegal activities and the insurance fraud he admitted to me he was involved in. It wasn't just theft of jewels and art. He arranged to have stocks and bonds stolen and then had sold.

Remember, I love you both so much. Remember too our special spot.

Uncle Timothy.

"What special spot, Riordan? I don't remember one."

"It's in his house, MaKenna. In the office. There was a spot on the shelf that he used to put your artwork and gifts. He was so proud of you two. I think he wanted you to remember that." Sarah blinked back tears as she rose. "I plan on visiting that house once more before I put it up for sale. I don't think any of us want to live there."

"There's one thing that I'm not clear on." MaKenna's words stopped them. "The house I bought. How did Uncle Timothy end up in that one?"

"He was friends with the owner. The owner was part of the group that ran with

Darby and was likely involved in the thefts and drugs. That's about all we can find out."

"That's likely a good idea." Ciaran rose and followed the group to the door, standing talking to them for a few minutes before he came back in, shutting and locking the door. He stood, his shoulder braced against the kitchen doorjamb, ankles crossed, as he watched MaKenna moving around the room.

"Well, love. It's over. Did you get all the answers you wanted?"

She shrugged. "I'm sure I have questions I haven't even thought of. I shudder to think of facing them in court in a few months." She looked up, fear in her eyes for a moment.

"We'll get through it, love. God will give us the strength. Now, what needs doing tonight?"

They worked away together, content in their silence, just happy to be with one another. Emma brushed up against as she stood behind them, in the way, but not budging.

Epilogue

Three months later, MaKenna stood in the backyard, Emma at her side, contemplating all the changes that had come into her life in the last six months or so. She knew Ciaran would be home shortly, but she needed some time just for her. They had decided to use her trust fund and set up scholarships for needy students and she was hard at work preparing that.

She turned in a circle, thinking back over the events she had faced. Not once had she dreamed with she opened the door that day to Ciaran when he came to clean up her yard that she would be married to him and serving God with him.

God had proven Himself to her in so many ways, she thought. Her favourite verses were those of a strong tower. She needed that daily reminder. Ciaran had found an old statue of a tower and brought it home to her one night. She smiled as she thought of his words to her that night.

She turned as Emma gave a low woof and ran for the house. Ciaran was home. Considering that he stated he hadn't liked dogs, Emma had won him over. Now, if she could convince him they needed a kitten, she would be content. But that would come she knew. She enjoyed how he courted her, bringing her flowers once a week, taking her out to dinner, for walks, just as he had promised.

She leaned back against him as he wrapped his arms around her. He had taken time to clean up from the dusty work he had been involved in.

"How was your day, love?" Ciaran's breath stirred the hair at her ears.

"Quiet. I finished the paperwork for the scholarships, spent some time with our Moms, and found a kitten."

"That sounds like a restful day." She waited, knowing at some point he would catch her words. "Hey, wait a moment. Kitten? What kitten?"

"Not yet, sweetheart. I just wanted to see if you really listened to me."

He turned her in his arms. "I do, love. Now, can I take my best girl out for pizza or something?"

She studied his face, seeing the lines that had developed during their adventure. "That would be lovely. Ciaran, thank you for being the man of God you are."

"And I could say thank you for being the lady God is changing every day." He raised his eyes to look around. "You've made some changes here?"

"Just a few. I know we talked about whether we would stay here or not, but for now, it's our home and I want it to reflect the changes and hope we have."

"That it does." His arm around her, he turned her towards the house. "I heard from Art today. The trial goes ahead in about a month. Are you up to testifying?"

She shrugged. "It's something we have to do. I know they have lots of evidence, but we need to say what we have to say. Darby affected our lives in ways he shouldn't have."

"That he did. Have you talked to Riordan lately?"

"Yes. And no, he hasn't found a girlfriend yet."

He nodded. "That's that, then." He waited for her response. "Something else is on your mind, isn't it?"

She nodded. "We've been so wrapped up in everything we've been through, we've missed talking about things we should have talked about before we married."

"Such as?"

"Oh, lots of things. Houses, furniture, pets, food, babies."

"No, we never talked about anything like that." He held the door for her and then followed her in. "Do you need to change or anything before we go out to eat?"

She shook her head, a smile on her face. He had missed the hint she had given him. Now, she would wait until he thought through what she had said.

Two hours later, he sat up in his office chair, finally hearing what she had said. He threw his pen down and went to find MaKenna. She was seated on the deck stairs, her eyes on the stars shining so brightly.

"MaKenna?"

"Yes, love?"

"What you said earlier, about what we hadn't talked about. You mentioned babies." He watched her face in the dusk, seeing when she turned towards him.

"Babies. Yes. We never talked about whether we wanted any children or not." Tears sparkled in her eyes even as a smile crossed her face. It had taken him long enough to hear her words.

"If God blesses us that way, love, then we will be blessed."

"Then, we'll be blessed, Ciaran. I think I want a little boy who looks just like."

"And I want a little girl just like you. How soon?"

"Not for a few months. We have time to plan and prepare."

He swept her into his arms and kissed her soundly, then sat, feeling suddenly overwhelmed until he remembered that God was there in each aspect of their lives and in this too.

"I think we'll keep this a secret just between us until we have to tell everyone."

"I quite agree, Ciaran. We'll have no peace once everyone knows."

He laughed and nodded. "I never thought that day we'd end up together, so much in love. God knew, didn't He? He's our strong tower, love, one that will never crumble or fall. He's provided that for us.

We just need to keep that in mind as we go through life."

"That we do, love. And I want to go on record stating that I hope we never ever have to face what we did or that anyone else we love has to. It's just too much."

Dear Readers:

A strong tower, something we all need to find at some point in our lives. Ciaran and Catriona certainly did, running from her father and his bodyguard, to safety and protection with God. It's a lifelong learning experience, to trust God enough to find that strong tower.

Emma, the Sheltie in the book, is absolutely based on my sable girl, Aberdale's Missy Emma Marie, call name Emma. Shelties are a wonderful breed, one you really have to know to appreciate. What Emma does in the book? My Emma does the very same. I also have two tri-coloured Shelties, Liam and Natalie, who mimic the book's Emma in so many ways.

The quickness of Ciaran and Catriona's wedding? Taken from close to real life. My parents had met in the fall of 1953 and were paired up to do evangelism by their minister. Ten weeks from the first time Dad walked Mom home, they were married, getting engaged on Valentinetine's day and married twelve days later. They had gotten to anniversary #56 when God called Mom home. Their lives reflected their love for one another and for God.

Thank you for picking up this story. It's been a challenge to write, hopefully enjoyable to you who read it.

God bless

Ronna